Lost Childhood

ANILAVA ROY

INDIA · SINGAPORE · MALAYSIA

Notion Press

Old No. 38, New No. 6
McNichols Road, Chetpet
Chennai - 600 031

First Published by Notion Press 2018
Copyright © Anilava Roy 2018
All Rights Reserved.

ISBN 978-1-64429-934-0

I dedicate this book to my beloved mother - late Gita Roy, who is no longer with me but will always be there in my thoughts

Contents

Introduction   *vii*

1. Background   1

2. Muzaffarpur   7

3. Allahabad (1968–1970)   11

4. Agra – (1970–1972)   23

5. Patna 1972 for 6 months   43

6. Ranchi – (1972 – 1974)   45

7. Patna (1974–1976)   71

8. Durgapur (1976–1978)   95

9. Bhubaneswar- (1978–1980)   105

10. Kolkata   139

Introduction

A thought has been brewing in my mind for a long time. I wanted to write about my childhood memories. The question that would always come in the mind of anyone is, "*Who am I?*"

I am not a celebrity, a film star, a cricketer, a politician or an industrialist. So, why am I writing this, what is its purpose and who is going to read this?

To me, 'childhood' is the best period a person can have after having traversed more than 50 years on this planet. Like many others of our era and our age, we have had sweet memories of childhood.

However, today's generation, i.e., our children, did not have the same kind of childhood as we had. I am hundred per cent sure that the generation which comes next will also not have our kind of childhood. The generation of people who were born in the late fifties, sixties and seventies would be the last of the generations to have this kind of a childhood

It is my attempt to bring that childhood to (a) our generation of people who can relive those memories, and to (b) our next generations who can, maybe, learn from them and see how one can be happy with little things in life. In a world where technology is growing at such speed, the world has become smaller. But, the distance between people has become bigger.

This is an attempt to pen those memories so that they are alive in some form as it will get lost perennially after our generation. It has been the case with the childhood of our parents and grandparents.

1. Background

Before I talk about myself, I will have to spend some time on my parents and explain what their background was and from where did they come from.

My father, Sisir Kumar Roy, was a banker. He came from a Zamindar family in Bangladesh. It is a big joke though that all Bengalis in Bangladesh were Zamindars. But, it was true. The British government had given the "Roy" title to them. My father's father, Late, Dinabandhu Roy, had a lot of land and also a liquor shop. My grandmother, Manorama Roy, was the 2nd wife to my grandfather. My Grandfather had 2 sons from the 1st wife and 2 sons and 2 daughters from his 2nd wife. My father was the youngest son, and after him, were the two sisters. My father's family came from a place called Comilla.

All wealth was lost during the build-up to independence during the British Raj. My eldest uncle lost the liquor shop, apparently, over a feud with the British. This shop was the source of a lot of revenue, and the family used to live comfortably on that.

My father used to study in Ishwar Pathshala. Later in his life, he would regale us with stories about the school and its teachers. It was one of the better schools in Comilla. My father was an average student who did reasonably well. My eldest uncle had the liquor shop which he lost. My 2nd eldest Uncle was very good in studies. He did his masters in Chemistry. He later migrated to Bombay (now Mumbai) and was with Raptakoss Bret and Co for many years. During his tenure with the company, he invented one of the most famous protein biscuits for pregnant women. This is one of the most popular medicinal biscuits even today. After his demise, my aunt also used to get the royalty for a long time.

The 3rd Uncle did his engineering and settled down in Jabalpur.

However, during his college days, my father was involved in the "*Swadeshi*" *Andolan* and was in the forefront. He had to go to prison very often. Much later, he was entitled to a grant which used to be given to all freedom fighters. However, he could not produce evidence of his prison stay in Bangladesh.

It was during those horrific days post-independence that my father came to Kolkata. In his words, they just had to leave with his mother and 2 sisters and had to come in one piece of cloth. The other uncles had already migrated to India by then.

The struggle in India started, and my father went over to Mumbai and joined a Bank called the "Comilla" Bank as a clerk. This bank was later renamed as the United Bank of India.

Out of my two aunts, one did her nursing course in Kolkata and became a nurse at the Ordnance factory hospital in Moradnagar. Later, she got married to someone she knew in the factory, and they settled down. They had children and lived there till their retirement.

My youngest aunt, *Choto Pisi*, did not study much and she got married to a person who used to work in the same bank as my father did. They settled in Bali in Howrah district.

Compared to my father's family, my mother came from a family which had been moderately rich and very educated. They originally belonged to Dacca, but they had come to Calcutta many years before the partition. This was a family of judges and advocates, and they were naturally very rich.

My grandfather, Jatindra Mohan Sarkar, was also an advocate. He was also a very good footballer, and he used to play regularly for the East Bengal Club. He was a sportsperson, tall and straight, even when he was close to 80.

However, his sons, my uncles or Mamas, did not have the sportsman in them which my mother had.

My eldest uncle, Rabindra Nath Sarkar, was a good student, and he became a Chartered Accountant. He joined the West Bengal government in the Finance department.

My youngest uncle, Bhaben Sarkar, did his MBBS from Nilratan Sircar Medical College. He wanted to do his MD from London. My grandfather had objected to it. But, my uncle insisted and went to London. He was never able to complete his MD, and he never came back to his country. He joined the National Health Department of UK and retired from there. He also never got married.

In contrast, my mother used to play a lot of sports. However, she was not in the same league as my grandfather. She studied only till class ten. She, however, could not pass as she got married to my father.

Many years later, my father used to joke about my mother's qualification. He would say that she was 'MABF-Matric appeared but failed!'

My mother, being a sportsperson she was, would take it in the right spirit and would give a fitting reply. We would all enjoy the family banter that we had.

We were "Bangals" as opposed to "Ghotis." The readers might wonder as to what it means. I am sure the Bengali readers would be able to relate to it. "Bangals" are people who are originally from the Eastern part of Bengal (now Bangladesh). "Ghotis" are from West Bengal. There has always been a tussle between these two sects over food, football and their nature.

Bengalis are passionate about their food and football. For us, we were passionate about food. But, we are not just limited to Bengali food, but we are passionate about all kinds of cuisine since we were more outside Bengal then inside it for a very long time. Also, since we were detached from Bengal and Kolkata for a long time, we were also detached to a great extent from the famous rivalry between "East Bengal "Club and Mohan Bagan Club. "Bangals" are die-hard supporters of East Bengal and "Ghotis" are of Mohan Bagan. This rivalry dates back to as early as May 1925 when they first met in a Calcutta League match. These 2 clubs have dominated not only the Kolkata football league but also the national football league for a long time.

So, when East Bengal won, the "Bangals "would have Illish or Hilsa cooked. When Mohan Bagan won, prawns were cooked. However, it did not mean that "Bangals" would not have prawns or "Ghotis" would not have *hilsas*. During those days, it was expected that all "Bangals" would support East Bengals while 100% of "Ghotis" would support Mohan Bagan.

As we were "Bangals" from both sides, we were supporters of East Bengal. However, we were never die-hard supporters of East Bengal. Since that attachment did not grow, we had a more nationalistic view supporting India on games like Hockey, cricket, etc.

That was the time in 1971 when one Sunil Gavaskar made his debut against the mighty West Indies and scored some 770 runs in the four-test series. India won the series under their captain Ajit Wadekar. The team again won for the first time in England. This was also largely due to the famous spin quartet of Bedi, Prasanna, Chandrasekhar and Venkat Raghavan.

We were connected to the world of cricket through the commentary we would hear on our one and only "Murphy" radio. During the Windies match, the commentary would be late in the night, and for the English match, it would be in the afternoon to late evening.

We Bangals were considered to be vocal in their views while "Ghotis" were supposed to be milder mannered. However, these are generic views.

Today, you will find a "Bangal" who is a supporter of "Mohan Bagan" and a Ghoti who is a diehard supporter of "East Bengal". As the world is becoming smaller, people are now fans and supporters of Liverpool and Manchester United. The rivalry between "Bangals" and "Ghotis" has lost its charm, and so has the rivalry between East Bengal and Mohan Bagan which has lost its passion and steam.

2. Muzaffarpur

I was born in 1965 in a place called Muzaffarpur. I was the youngest amongst the 4 brothers. I also had a sister who was the oldest. However, she died soon after she was born. My 3 elder brothers were born in a place called Kodarma in Bihar. My father, after his stint in Mumbai, got married, and then, he started moving from one place to another. He started from Giridih, from where he moved to Kodarma and then to Muzaffarpur.

All 3 of my brothers had an age gap of 2 years each, and I had a difference of 3 years. I was in Giridih when my father came close to another family - Mr. Kalyan Ghosh who had a mica business. It was a flourishing business. Mr. Kalyan Ghosh or Jethu, as we called him, had 3 sons and 2 daughters as well. Since my father was newly married and my mother was new to the place, Jethima (wife of Kalyan Ghosh) would take very good care of my mother.

Before my parents were in Giridih, they had also been to a place called Kodarma in Bihar, at that point in time.

This is the place where all my elder brothers were born. This is the place where another lifelong friendship was formed with another family- the Pandit family. Pandit **Jethu was my father's colleague,** and they helped settle our family settle when they were in Kodarma.

Jethu (uncle) had two sons and one daughter. The eldest son became a doctor, and the youngest son (Shymalda) joined the same bank as Jethu and Father. Those days, one son could get an employment in the same bank. However, this policy was discontinued in 1971 with the nationalisation of banks. Uncle had a daughter as well who was the youngest. This tie still lasts even after 60 long years. However, the ties have weakened considerably now.

The bonding with the Ghosh family though grew with time, and the relationship became very strong and went on for more than 50 years. It resulted in the two families coming together. My eldest brother got married to the youngest daughter of their family.

My eldest brother is Amitava Roy, just after him is Asitava Roy and just above me is Arunava Roy.

Before I go on, let me just talk about Muzaffarpur.

Muzaffarpur, my birthplace, was a small city. It is actually a sub-metro city situated on Burhi Gandak River. The city was established way back in 1875 by the British. Muzaffarpur is famous for lychees, and it is meeting place of Hindu and Islamic thoughts and culture. Dr Rajendra Prasad, the first Indian President of India, hailed from this place.

I was born in a Christian Missionary Hospital which was run by the foreigners. Since I was born early in the morning, the sister in the hospital named me "Prabhat Kiran."

However, this name did not stay, and I was later called Anilava Roy - a name which was in sync with the names of my elder brothers.

I was very sickly from the time I was born. I could not eat much. Soon after 2 years of my birth, my sister was born.

My father loved girls, but as destiny would have it, she also did not stay long. She died after 6 months in Calcutta Medical College where my youngest Uncle was an intern at that time. She died of a rare disease. She was a beautiful child. My memories of her were from the photograph which was there at the time of "*Annaprasan*" where she looked heavenly. But, she was destined to stay with us only for a short time.

I do not have many memories of Muzaffarpur. While I was 2 or 3 years old (1969), my father was transferred to Allahabad.

3. Allahabad (1968-1970)

Allahabad is a great city with historical and political significance. This was originally known as Prayag or "the city of offering," and is the confluence or *Sangam* of three major rivers of Ganga, Jamuna and Saraswati. It is the 2nd oldest city after Banaras.

In an early 17th century, Allahabad was the provincial capital of the Moghul Empire under the reign of Emperor Jehangir. According to Akbarnama, Emperor Akbar laid the foundation of the city of Prayag. This was later renamed as "Allahabad" by Emperor Shah Jahan.

The city is famous for many religious and cultural events; the most popular being the Kumbh Mela.

I still remember that we stayed in a place called Civil Lines. This is the most central place in Allahabad. It was built in 1857 by the British, and it was the largest township built before the city of Delhi.

We used to stay in a flat in a high-rise building. My brothers were admitted to Boys High School which is, still today, one of the most famous schools in Allahabad. It was built in 1861 by the British to provide Christian education to the Europeans and the British. But, it accepted children from all backgrounds.

Initially a co-ed school, it, later on, became a Boys School.

It would be of interest to all to know that Mr. Amitabh Bachchan was also a student of this school from class 1 to class 7.

I was also part of this school but for only a day! The day I was admitted to the school, my father got transferred again.

I would probably be the only student of Boys High School who studied in that school for 1 day! You might want to check Guinness Book of World Records for that. I was just joking!

My father always wanted to give the best education to his children at any cost, and he would send his children to the best of the schools. We were very fortunate to have gone to the most premier of schools in each city.

There used to be a big playground around our house, and we would play there every day. We were joined by the waiters of the Coffee House which was just near the playground. While playing cricket, if the ball was hit strongly, it would fly into the main road.

The one thing which we inherited from our mother was the sporting genes, and all 4 brothers loved to play.

While I was small, and my participation was limited. However, going forward, I would play all kind of sports along with my brothers. In both indoors and outdoors, we excelled in some of them. It would include outdoor games like cricket, hockey, football, basketball, kabaddi, kho-kho, badminton, gully danda, and also indoor games such as table tennis. We would play tennis on our dining table with books placed in the middle of the table to act as the net! Of course, we would play other indoor games like Chess, Ludo, Chinese checkers, cards, book cricket, etc.

I am not sure whether all my readers would be familiar with all the games, especially the game of "Gully danda."

I have not seen this game being played at all nowadays.

It is a simple game played between 2 teams. It requires only 2 things - one large stick (danda) and a smallish stick with one side narrowed (gully). A hole is created in the ground, and the gully is placed in a horizontal position over the hole in the ground. With the help of the long stick, one player has to hit it with all possible strength. There would be players to catch it. If they caught the gully, then the player was out. However, they if they could not, then the opposing team member had to throw it down and hit the long stick placed near the hole. If they could hit, the player was out.

However, if they did not manage to hit the long stick, then the attacking team member would get the chance to hit the gully thrice. The idea was to hit it as hard and as further as possible. There was also a technique to hit the "Gully." You would need first to strike the gully at its narrow end so that the gully would bounce up in the air. As it bounced in the air, you would need to hit it as hard as you could.

The opposing team members had to now throw the Gully from wherever it had reached to hit to the long stick. Then, the 2nd team would get a chance to be the attacker and so on and so forth.

My father was an extremely busy and a very serious kind of a person. I was extremely petrified of him, and so were my brothers. He was a workaholic person who only thought about his work. His branch was a loss-making branch, and he was sent there specifically to turn it around. He toiled hard, had to take a lot of tough decisions, made innovative changes and made it a profitable branch in 2 years' time. I remember that Baidyanth was one of the prime customers of that Branch and they used to respect my father a lot. We even went to their residence as well on some occasions. However, it took a toll on my father. He used to come back late every day with thousands of worries, and he used to be in a foul mood.

We have witnessed 2 incidents which made me fear my father more.

On one such occasion, in one of the evenings, after we came back home post our cricket match, there was a serious altercation with some of the boys. These were Punjabi boys who were from the same building. They got into an argument with my 2nd brother (Asitava). Now he was always an ill-tempered person. Very soon they started trading blows with each other. That guy's brother also got into the brawl. Seeing that, my eldest brother also got into the act. Very soon, my brother duo started beating them up. They ran away after getting bruised and beaten badly.

We also came back home quietly after that; though I was scared. We thought everything was over. We quickly went to our room, and my brothers started studying. I was not going to school at that point in time, and I could hear the bell ringing. I opened the door to see my father walking in. As usual, he was tired and not in a very good mood.

At the same moment, the tutor of my brothers had also come. Immediately there was another ring on the door. As my mother opened the door, the mother of the boys whom my brothers had beaten up had come to complain!

As luck would have it, my father had come early on that day, and he heard what the boy's mother had to say. She complained about how my brothers had nearly killed them, and how we should teach them etc.

On one hand, he was tired, and on the other hand, he did not expect to hear the complaint.

He apologised profusely to the lady and closed the door. He was fuming with anger. Seeing that, my 2nd brother, Mejda, smartly went to the tutor and started studying.

My Dada, he was not as smart as my Mejda was in front of my father. My father quickly took out the wire of the Iron and started beating up Borda badly. So much so that his legs had the mark of the bruises. My mother started crying and the rest us were petrified.

Much later in the night, when Borda was asleep, I could see my father putting Boroline on the legs of my Borda. The fatherly love was evident from this action.

My father was/is extremely fond of Borda, and I am sure that after beating him, my father could not have forgiven himself.

There was another incident. When my father came late as usual after a hard day's work as well as a day which was full of issues, he sat for dinner along with all of us. It was a practice in our house that everybody would come to the dinner table and have dinner together. This was maintained all throughout as we grew up.

During that night, my mother started cribbing about something. My mother had this bad habit of continuing with the same thing over and over again until it became irritating.

She was blabbering as usual when suddenly my father threw the plate across the table, and it landed near the kitchen!

Everybody was dumbfounded. My mother started crying, and she went on crying. We did not know how to react. Everybody went to sleep including my father. However, my mother took me, went to the Puja room and sat there crying. Maybe I was crying too. I do not remember how long we were there in the Puja room, how long I was awake or how long was father awake.

It was in Allahabad that my father bought a gramophone from HMV. That was a great day for us. All this while, we had a Murphy radio, and our world was limited and restricted to it. For a long time, I believed that there were people inside the radio who were actually talking, and singing! In fact, once I went behind the radio to check, but I could not find anyone.

We bought many LP records Like Hemant Mukhopadhyaya, Shyamal Mitra and many records in both Hindi and Bengali. I used to like the songs of Shyamal Mitra in particular. Later on, we would buy many records like Disco Diwane, Kishore Kumar and many others.

It was in Allahabad that Chandeswar Mahato came into our family. He was a boy of 14 who had come from Bihar, and he was a few years older than my eldest brother. He used to work in our house and help my mother doing household chores. However, he was a hard-working person. He wanted to study and do well in his life. So, he would study my brother's books in his spare time. He was very sincere and honest - qualities you would not find with today's people. He considered himself to be the eldest son of my father and changed his title from Mahato to Roy!

My father got him to work as a peon on a temporary basis in his bank.

I still remember I had once gone to see a movie with him, and it was Mera Naam Joker. We had sat on the first row and watched the movie. I still remember a few scenes even today after almost 50 years.

During those days in Allahabad, I also remember having seen the iconic Satyajit Ray film- Gopi Gayen, Bagha Bayen. That was the first time we were introduced to the films of the maestro. Over the years, we would watch his other creations.

Since Allahabad was a holy place, a lot of relatives would come and visit us. My maternal grandfather (Dadu), my maternal uncles, our cousins, my paternal uncles and aunts. All of them wanted to visit and take a dip in the holy Prayag. We would also frequent the Holy Ganges and just sit there to enjoy the serenity.

However, my Grandfather's visit had its own issues. He would come and visit every place where my father got transferred to his last day.

My grandfather (Dadu) was a very strict one person and a strict disciplinarian very similar to my father. We would not call our elder brothers "dada", and that is something which is criminal in Bengali family. I would only call my eldest brother as "dada" whereas I would address the other two brothers by their nicknames. This had become acceptable in our family. We would also speak in both Hindi and Bengali, (Hindi mostly) and that was also unthinkable for others.

Hence, whenever Dadu would come, we would mark the calendar with the day when he was supposed to leave.

However, we also looked forward to the money he would give each one of us when he left, and it would be a crisp new 5 Rupee note. That was a very big amount in those days.

My youngest maternal uncle would also come and visit. We also used to look forward to his visits. He came from England, and he would bring a lot of gifts for all of us. However, over a period of time, his gifts would gradually become less and less attractive. I still remember on his first visit, he had given a Meccano to my eldest brother. You can make stuff like planes, cranes, etc., with it. It was so apt since my brother became a mechanical engineer in his life. He had also brought a camera toy with circular films inside it, and there was a switch to change the slide. It was beautiful, and I still remember that there was a Peter Pan story in one of the discs. It was so lively that it seemed as if it was a 3D picture. I do not remember as to what he had bought for my other brother or me.

I also have very fond memories of another game he had bought for my cousins in Kolkata, and it was Monopoly. When we used to go to Calcutta, (now Kolkata) we would spend a lot of time playing Monopoly with our cousins. It was an interesting game, and we would spend hours on the same. We also had very few opportunities to go outside and play. Neither would our Uncles take us out. It was only when father came along we would go and visit the Zoo, see the puppet show and watch movies. Of course, he used to get sarees for Ma, and these were mainly chiffon.

My memory about Allahabad is blurred, but I still remember a day when my father came back from office. That was the day when I had gone to school for the first time. He told me that I need not go to the school anymore since he was now getting transferred to Agra, and it was time to pack up and go.

From here on, we would move from one city to another. We would stay for 2 years, and then, again move to another city. Once, Father got transferred after just 6 months.

However, I must give credit to my mother. While Father would go and join the office in the new city, it would be Mother who would take care of all the packing, have the goods loaded in the truck and then finally move with her children in a train to a new city. Those days, you did not have the packers. A few guys would come with bags, and they would put things like almirahs, tables, etc., in big bags and have them stitched. It was a time taking activity and required a lot of supervision. Then, of course, we went to schools and got transfer certificates. In many cases, we studied in different schools.

At the same time, Father would reach the new city, look for a rented place, and also, look for schools. As I mentioned earlier, he never compromised on education, and he always got us into the best schools.

However, it was also a fact that within those 2 years or three years of our stay, we would invariably change our house once, since we never liked the first house. It is also a fact that we stayed in big houses in most cities, and in most cases, bungalows.

For us, it was exciting to have an opportunity to see another city, go to another school and make new friends.

In my life, till class VIII, my father was transferred 8 times!

I still wonder how many of our generation will be willing to relocate the entire family so many times and so frequently. Even if they get transferred, they keep their families in the same city and move alone to the new city for multiple reasons including children's study, parents cannot move, etc.

However, my father never thought of that as an option, and staying in different cities was unthinkable. Staying together as a family was the norm.

It did have its impact on us. Especially on our schooling. To me particularly because, when my father would get transferred mid-session, we would not get admission in the new city mid-way.

I did lose a couple of years on account of that. However, when I look back and see, it hardly matters if you are late by a couple of years; you work for a couple of years less. In fact, I could not continue working till retirement age even after losing 2 years!

Among other things which were impacted, we could never create the friendship bond that we normally do when we study in the same school for several years. Here, we were only there for 2 years, and then, we moved to another city for another stint of 2 years. We would not build up the lifelong school friendships which others do. However, now at this age, when technology is with you, you can connect with lost friends. But, I guess, it does not have the same bonding.

However, what we lost was more than made up for with the rich and varied experience we gathered about people and places in the subsequent years.

This was something which no school can teach you.

4. Agra (1970-1972)

It was time to move on. We packed our bags and baggage and moved to the city of Taj Mahal.

Agra, famously known as the city of Taj, is a great tourist attraction in India and is of great historical significance. It is located on the banks of river Yamuna and is situated very close to Delhi. It has many tourist attractions like the Taj Mahal which is considered to be one of the seven wonders of the world, the Agra Fort and the Fatehpur Sikri. The city first finds mention in the Epic "Mahabharata" where it was known as Agrevava meaning "the border of the forest."

Sikander Lodhi was the first Emperor to shift his capital from Delhi to Agra. His son Ibrahim Lodhi ruled for nine years till he was defeated by Babur in the first battle of Panipat. From 1540 to 1556, it was ruled by the Afghans beginning with Sher Shah Suri. It was the capital of the Moguls from 1556 to 1658

As I mentioned, we first moved into a small house, but we moved out of the house to a bigger house. It was a single-storeyed house. However, it was segregated into 4 parts, and in each part, there were 4 tenants. Outside the house, there was a huge driveway where one could use the same for playing games like Kabaddi. There was also a huge garden in the front where all tenants could assemble on various occasions. The new house was situated in Wazirpur.

The first task my father had was to get his four sons admitted in school, and as I had mentioned earlier, Father would take all efforts to put us into very good schools.

However, we had to be admitted into 3 different schools.

My eldest brother (dada) was admitted at St Peters College. The school was founded in 1846. It is one of the oldest convent schools in the country. The college reached such prominence by 1870 that the then visiting Inspector wrote in his report that it "bear(s) no unfavourable comparison with the best institutions of a similar kind in England and Europe."

In the same year, the school was affiliated to Calcutta University for its first entrance examination, and was henceforth called "College." Education in St Peters was considered to be a sure passport to the Roorkee Engineering College, various government departments, secretariats, etc. Because of the high reputation of the college, dignitaries like Prince of Wales, the Duke and Duchess of Connaught, The Duke of Edinburg, Lord Rippon, Governor of Uttar Pradesh, Mother Teresa, leading sportsperson like Vijay Hazare, Milkha Singh, P.T.

Usha and Kapil Dev have visited the school in different times.

My second brother, Mejda, got admitted to St Georges College. It is also one of the oldest English Medium Schools in India. It is located in Mall Road and was established in 1875. It was opened mainly for the children of European armed forces. Later on, it started accepting children from other strata of the society. The students of this school were known as Georgians.

So far as my Sejda and I were concerned, we were admitted into a primary school known as St Francis. This was again a convent school which was established in 1957. The first batch of class X happened only in 1997.

Agra was not as congested as it is now. We all know that Agra is known amongst the many historical monuments including the Taj Mahal, one of the Seven Wonders of the World. We have been fortunate to see Taj on many occasions, in various seasons, early morning, afternoon, evening, in the night and in full moon. Each time it was a new feeling even at the tender age. We saw it as a family, we saw it along with various relatives who came from Kolkata, Delhi and Mumbai. We saw it with father's colleagues. Post that, I have seen Taj Mahal with my family. However, I have not enjoyed because of the huge crowd and the serpentine queue which one has to endure.

We never waited in a queue at the Taj during those days. You could really laze around and enjoy the beauty. There were times when we would just laze around the garden surrounding the Taj and not go to the main monument. Another historical monument is the Agra Fort, from where Shah Jahan was kept captive by his son Aurangzeb. From his "Jharkhand," one can see the Taj clearly. The fort is a magnificent symbol of Mughal Grandiose with the rooms of Jahanara and Roshanara which are in the shape of a palanquin. The fountains inside the rooms and the huge courtyards are a testimony to the wealth and pomp of the Moghuls.

However, another historical monument which attracted me then and even now is Fatehpur Sikri. The huge Buland Darwaja is so imposing that one feels so small in its presence. Nowadays, one does not enter through the Buland Darwaja as one could do so at that point in time.

I still remember the road from Agra to Fatehpur Sikri. It was narrow and desolate. On both sides of the road, there was a dense jungle. One would visit the monument in either morning or afternoon and come back early. Nobody would risk coming through that road in the evening or night.

Once, very senior people from the Head Office of father's bank from Kolkata had visited Agra. They had come on a business cum pleasure trip. If my memory goes right, the MD and the GM of the bank, along with their wives, had visited. Though they stayed in a hotel, they were invited to our house for lunch and dinner. They obviously visited Taj and did a lot of shopping

One of the things which they wanted to do was to visit Fatehpur Sikri in the night. They were inspired by the

Bengali movie of Khudita Pashan inspired on the story of Rabindra Nath Tagore. There was a scene in the movie which was shot on a dark night in the fort.

It was decided that we will go there after dinner in the full moon. So, they all went in an Ambassador along with Father and Mother. I was taken along since I would accompany mother most of the times she would go on a trip. The car sped in the narrow road between the dense jungle, and we reached.

It was a beautiful sight seeing the imposing Buland Darwaja in the full moon. At the same time, it looked desolate, and the feeling was eerie. I sat back in the car along with the driver while our guests along with Baba and Ma started climbing the steps of the Buland Darwaja into the fort.

After what seemed ages, I could see them coming, moving down the stairs. I was feeling very sleepy but was afraid of being alone in the car. I was happy to see them come back.

We started our journey back to Agra. It was completely desolate, and there was not a soul on the road. As the car sped through the road, I could feel that the elders were now scared. It was rumoured that there were dacoits in the jungle surrounding the road. After travelling for about 15 minutes, the car suddenly stopped.

The father asked the driver as to what the issue was. It seemed that car had run out of fuel!

That was it! All hell broke loose. How could the driver be so irresponsible that he would not check the fuel? The ladies in the car were now shouting at the driver. At the same time, fear was lurking inside the car. Where would the driver get the fuel? There was no petrol pump in sight. There was no one in sight on the road as well.

The driver finally got out of the car and took a can to go and look for petrol. There was no other alternative or choice.

The real problem started then. The ladies were wearing ornaments. They started taking them out and kept them in their purses.

However, the fear was palpable. While it was a full moon, there were no lights in the road. It seemed like an eternity that the driver had gone, and the patience was breaking. The door of the car was locked from the inside.

Finally, after what seemed an eternity, the driver came back. He had managed to get about 2 litres of fuel from another car. After pouring the diesel, the car finally started.

Everybody sighed with relief, and we reached home. This was an experience that I would never forget.

I again visited Agra in 2017. I also went to see Fatehpur Sikri. The road was big. There are habitats across the road on both sides, and there was no jungle anymore. There are hotels and restaurants all across, and again a sea of humanity near the Fort.

Another fascinating monument or temple which a lot of tourists do not visit is the Dayalbagh Temple. It is the *Samadhi* of Radha Swami, and it has been built in the basement. It was built with pure white marble brought from Makrana, green stones for Baroda and yellow stones from Jaisalmer. There are intricate carvings of different fruits and vegetables across the temple. When we visited the temple, we could see many workers still working in various parts of the temple. It was not complete even after years. Even today, after 113 years, it is still not completed! It is rumoured that it is designed never to be completed which the *Sangha* denies. According to them, the temple would be completed in Dec 2018 on the occasion of the 200th birth anniversary of the founder. They are expecting 5 lac followers to come. The current workers are 5th generation workers who are working on this temple. The initial workers used to work on Rs 2 per day. Now, the current workers get 400 to 500 Rs per day.

One may never know the truth. But that is how it is, and a temple never got completed even after 113 years!

Since our school was near, my Sejda (elder brother) and I used to go by rickshaw. My Dada and Mejda would go by a school bus as their schools were far off from our house.

In Agra, my father bought a gas oven and a cylinder for the first time. Before that, mother used to cook on something we used to call "*Chullah*" which was lit with coke and cow dung cake. It was a boon for Mother since she did not have to spend so much time on igniting the *Chullah*.

Having said that, we were always fortunate to have full-time maids and servants. My mother always had them at her beck and call!

This was also the time when father bought the first proper dining table. The cover was white sun mica with light shades of grey. I remember this design was taken from the dining table of the Taj Express train's dining table which used to travel between Agra and Delhi! We all wanted that design, and so we got it. We used to have a great time going to school, playing games, doing all kinds of mischief, watching movies on Sundays.

Father used to take us out on Sundays. If we were not going to visit monuments, we were going for the movies. In fact, he used to take us to all famous Hollywood movies of the time. However, we also saw a lot of these movies when we used to come to Calcutta (now Kolkata).

We saw movies like Patton, The Good, the bad and the Ugly, How the west was won, McKenna's Gold, Sound of Music, etc. We also watched many Hindi movies. One of them which I remember having seen was Lalkar, which was a war movie.

Talking about war, we witnessed the 1971 war with Pakistan from close quarters.

It was in Dec 1971 that the war was declared. However, during that time, I did not understand the reason for war or its impact. I was not even aware that time it was about the liberation of East Pakistan (now Bangladesh). I am not sure whether my brothers were aware or not.

To me or to us, it meant that we did not have to go to schools for those days.

The war started with the Pakistani Air Force initiating the process of bombing various Indian airfields including Agra. So, Agra had become the target of the Pakistani Air Force.

Blackout order was issued in Agra. This meant that nobody would venture out of their house post evening – say, 5 pm. All the windows were pasted with black sheets of paper so that no light could come out of the house.

We used to finish our dinner by 6 pm and go to bed. All lights would be switched off. Imagine going to bed by 6 pm!

It so happened, that one day, my brother was changing, and he had not switched off the lights post 5 pm. My father scolded and told him to go to bed directly without changing. He did not have pants on, and he went to bed in the same way!

In the evening, we would see the fire of gunshots, and immediately, we would see flickers of light in the sky just like we see during Diwali from the firecrackers in the sky. It was nothing but Pakistani aircraft being brought down by anti-aircraft guns of the Indian Army.

The Pakistan Air Force attempt to bomb Agra airfield was largely unsuccessful. Since, by that time, all aircrafts had been moved out. On the contrary, their aircraft were brought down by Indian anti-aircraft guns.

The Pakistani Air Force also bombed Agra City. We could hear the sounds during the night, and we used to be very scared. We always used to pray that bombs should not fall anywhere near our house.

In the daytime, we saw a huge crater which had been created in the marketplace. It was very near to our house, and hence, the danger was real and very near.

It was during this time that Taj Mahal was covered and camouflaged so that it would not be visible to the Pakistani Air Force. It was done more for not providing the Pakistani Air Force with an opportunity to identify Agra rather than to protect the Taj. I do not know whether this is true, but that is what some people said.

Finally, the war came to an end. India completely decimated Pakistan, and they were forced to surrender publicly. It led to the creation of a new country-Bangladesh. Pakistan never forgot this humiliation and waged war with India in years to come.

There was a Sikh in our premises whose son had gone to the war. When he came back, I remember having gone to their house. He was a lieutenant in the Indian army and had gone to the western frontier to fight. We heard stories from him as to how they did not take out their shoes for more than 10 days and how their they escaped death from artillery fire. He also showed us the empty artillery cartridges which he had brought.

That was the first time we were face to face with an Indian soldier, and that is how we first started respecting

Indian armed forces who they lay down their lives to protect us.

That family had a tradition of all generations going to the Armed forces, and he was the latest generation to have joined armed forces and go to the frontier.

I was the youngest, and hence, I was protected by my mother. However, I was bullied at times by my brothers in a playful manner.

I remember that Ma used to prepare Egg curry. Those days in our family, it was not the full egg which we used to get, but a half egg. I was very close to my Sejda. I used to go to school with him, and I would sleep with him. If I needed to go to the bathroom, he would accompany me since I was scared of the darkness.

He would take a price for that! He would demand a share of half the egg after having his share! He would also demand a cut in the daily money which we got, and so on so forth. This went on for a long time. Though my Mejda would offer help at the same price, I would not trust him so much. So, Sejda was the better of the 2 evil forces!

I was also used as a ball to be thrown between 2 beds! As I was very light in weight, two of my brothers would take turns to throw me from one bed to another. My brother would catch me in the bed across the room. They managed to do this very well. However, there would be times when I would just fall on the edge of the bed. Thankfully nothing ever happened!

In any case, Mejda (elder brother) had a very bad temper. When he would lose it, he used to become violent and difficult to control.

Once, we are playing Kabaddi in the premises' *veranda*. All my brothers, along with the other children, were part of it. It started raining, and my mother was calling all of us inside the house. Then, suddenly, an altercation happened between Dada and Mejda. Before we realised, Mejda ran into the house, got the "*dau*" (a kitchen knife) and ran after Ma to kill her!

He was somehow restrained. He had this violent streak inside him. My Dada was stronger, and he would always beat up Mejda in a physical battle.

Chandeswar, who was with us for a very long time and was working on a temporary basis, finally became permanent in the bank and was posted out of Agra. He, finally, left our house and embarked on his journey. He used to write letters giving father all the information. He also enquired about us. He also got married and had children. We last saw him in 1984 when he came to Kolkata to meet us. He took us out for a movie and treated us. That was the last we saw of him, and we have never met up since then. I am not sure whether he is alive today. If he is, he would be around 70 to 75 years old. I am sure his children would have been married, and so would have been his grandchildren.

As expected, we had many people visiting us in Agra from relatives to friends to Father's office colleagues. We used to have many visitors throughout the year, and it was good fun. We would also accompany them in their visits to Taj Mahal and other historical places. However, even after seeing Taj Mahal so many times and in different seasons, at different times of the day, one is never bored. Every time, its sheer magnificence, and its beauty mesmerises you. Even at a tender age, we could feel it, and such was its grandeur.

However, apart from visiting the historical monuments, Agra was a shopper's paradise. From marble to leather goods, from the famous "*Nagra*" shoes to "Dye and tie" sarees and of course, the famous *pethas* were bought at Agra.

As with the others, marble items like vases and ornamental boxes were bought, and of course, the miniature "Taj Mahal" in a glass box with lighting inside it. It was a must buy for all visitors. and We had also bought many of them in different shapes and hues. However, unfortunately, none of them is there anymore. While you can still buy them and buy them in many places, we never bought after that. It is also said that buying a Taj Mahal is not considered auspicious since the Taj is built on a *Maqbara* or a grave!

My mother had a huge collection of *Nagra* shoes as well as Tie and dye sarees. Tie and dye sarees were originally from Jaipur (Rajasthan).

Of course, none of the visitors forgot to take *Petha*. *Petha* had originated in Agra. According to some, it has its origin in the kitchen of the Mughal emperor Shah Jahan.

It is a sweet which is made from ash gourd, or in simple terms, white pumpkin. It comes in different flavours like *Kesar Petha, angoori petha, pan petha* and many others.

Agra was and is also famous for stone studded jewellery, brass items and leather items like belts and bags.

Mother again had a huge number and variety of bags. Even my Dada had a fetish for belts. In those days, it was the large broad belts with engravings on it. In many cases, you would have names of Hindi movies engraved on them!

Now, you have a lot of world-class hotels since Agra is the go-to destination of not only foreign tourists but also domestic tourists. At that time, there were not too many.

I still remember one *Clark Shiraz*. The reason I remember is that my parents had gone there multiple times. These were parties hosted by large clients of the bank. It was a five-star luxury hotel, and my simple mother would be overawed by these occasions. While she did not know English, she was smart and would manage. On one occasion, she had worn the *Nagra*. According to her, the carpet was so soft, that the *Nagra* went inside the carpet.

She was not adept in eating with fork and knife. Hence, she would probably take a Nan with some dal and nibble on it!

We always used to tell her, "You are wasting such good foods by not eating them." But, she was ok.

Father used to drink once in a while, but never at home. We first got to see him drunk after returning from one such party We were told later that his drinks were mixed!

While in Agra, we would also travel to Hardwar and Delhi.

Father had taken my grandmother as well. We went together to the holy place. My only remembrance of Hardwar at that point in time is the Lakshman Jhula across river Ganges in Rishikesh. It is an iron suspension bridge which connects two villages of Tapovan in Tehri Garhwal district on the west bank of the river, to Jonk, in Pauri in Garhwal District.

We also went to Delhi. In Delhi, all my father's cousins from my grandmother's side were based. Father had 5 cousins who were all in Delhi. We would go and stay with them, and our Uncles would take us to many places in Delhi including Lal Qila, India Gate, Qutub Minar and Rashtrapati Bhawan.

I always find Lal quila fascinating. It took us back to the Moghul period and the various upheavals it would have witnessed. Especially, fascinating was the sound and light programme in Lal Qila which used to portray events of history.

We would also visit our *Boro Pishi's* (Aunt) house in Moradnagar. My *Pisha* (Uncle) used to work as a foreman in the ordinance factory, and my aunt used to work in the ordinance factory hospital as a nurse. While the quarter was small and there was nothing to see in Moradnagar, my father would still visit. I guess that is how the bonding was created.

No matter how well we are connected with each other on the social network, if we do not see each other, somewhere, the bonding goes off, and that is what is happening today. In fact, as brothers, we do not see each in years, and somewhere, the bonding had loosened. It is sad and unfortunate.

That is why our fathers and forefathers insisted on meeting at least once in 2 years if not one. People would find time for it.

My Pisha (Uncle) had two children. One son and one daughter. Shankar was the son who was a year younger to my Dada and Mita (daughter) was a year younger to me. Of course, our regular visits to Mama's house (maternal Uncle's Place) in Calcutta would continue.

We used to hate going to their place. Personally speaking, I never used to feel the warmth there. Usually, children in our time loved going to their maternal place. But, it was never the case with us. We would find out, in our many visits, then and later that we were always considered inferior.

However, Ma would go there since *Dadu* was there. My uncles would consider all of us very rustic except my Dada who was their favourite. I have a feeling that they did not have a great opinion of my father as well. In various occasions, they would make fun of him. However, my father would never react. He always used to laugh it away. However, they knew that my father had risen in his career and was doing reasonably well, considering the fact that he came from a humble background and he was not as educated as they were. He was an ordinary pass graduate while they were chartered, accountants and doctors. The rest of us were called "Khottas" which was a term loosely used to call Biharis. It was, maybe, because we used Hindi as well apart from Bengali. However, they forgot that we were going to premium Christian missionary schools in each city.

Also, we had nowhere to go once in Calcutta. Our day would begin with a cup of horrible milk which had a peculiar stink. Then, the breakfast would always be aloo *sabji* and rotis. Lunch and dinner were also equally abysmal. The only saving grace was the time spent with our cousins Suman and Joy. Suman was the same age as my next brother, and Joy was younger to me. They were both good at studies, and they went to South Point School. They eventually became engineers. Today, they are working in West Bengal State Electricity Board and Oil India respectively and are well settled in life.

We used to play all indoor games like monopoly and spend time likewise. We were never taken outdoors by our Mamas.

It was only when father would come he would take us out see movies like Sound of Music and Ben Hur. He also took us to The Birla Planetarium, Indian Museum, the Zoo and the puppet show.

One thing which we liked while coming to Calcutta was the ride from the Howrah station to Tollygunge where our uncle stayed. We would get down and ride the double-decker bus no 6. We would immediately go upstairs and sit right in front. The bus would take more than an hour traversing through the city, and we would alight at Ranikuthi (Tollygunge).

Double-decker bus was introduced by the British in 1926, and it has a lot of nostalgia associated with it. Many years later, in the 1990s, the left-front government would slowly phase out the double-decker buses since they were considered unsuitable for Calcutta traffic. It seems that they are going to come back on the roads of Kolkata! As they say, old things have the habit of coming back!

If one was in Agra, and if you were there during Holi, it is a different feeling. We got out the taste of Holi the way it was played in Uttar Pradesh. People of Uttar Pradesh have a certain way- *tahjeeb*. They are well educated and very cultured people. They are very courteous people and people with a fine way of speaking. Their Hindi is chaste and totally different from the way it is spoken in, say, Bihar.

Before the day of Holi, we would all assemble in the big garden to celebrate *Holika Dahan*. The burning of the evil Holika is celebrated as Holi. He was killed by Lord Vishnu in order to save Prahalad his devotee. A lot of bamboo pieces are used to be lit. The bonfire would be lit. Everybody would gather around and wait till the bonfire was doused out.

The next day, we would dress in old clothes and play with colours and sprays. We would never throw colours at our elders. No bad material or oil colour would be used. In the afternoon, the elders would go and visit their friends' place and have bhang which would be mixed with "*Thandais*" and sweets. But, as children, we would not be allowed to have all that.

The bright colours of our stay in Agra were coming to an end, and it was time to move again after another 2 years. This time, it was to Patna, the capital of Bihar at that time. It was time to pack our bags and baggage once again. It was time to take a transfer certificate from each school and move on.

The journey in Agra had ended. While we would come back later as adults with our own families, it was never the same again.

5. Patna 1972 for 6 months

This stint was the shortest for 6 months! This was incredible. Even with our standard of 2 to 3 years, this was short. I would not know what the reasons for father were to get transferred after only six months. He is alive today, but I guess he is so old to be able to remember. I also do not know as to why he would agree to such frequent transfers. We all know that people in PSU banks get transferred, but not at these frequencies. I think we all took it in our stride.

None of us took the loss of a year seriously. This would not be the case today. I have seen families staying in 2 different cities for years because the harm it would do to the child's education. It is no longer 'children' as most parents today have one child, and at the most, two. Nobody today would be able to imagine the scenario then. We were like wanderlust or wanderers in a family way. New cities, new homes, new schools, new friends, new food, new places and a new culture.

My own brother in law has been transferred to Mumbai, and he is staying alone while his wife and son continue to stay in Kolkata. This is for not hampering the studies of the son. While I agree that education and studies are important, somehow, the bond does not stay very strong.

While not everyone would agree, they would say that long distance relationships can remain strong. Well, it is my opinion, and others may be right as well.

We did get inducted into new schools. We stayed in a flat in a place called Rajendra Nagar. It was one of the premium locations at that time in Patna. However, since the stay was for 6 months, I have not much to write about this stint.

It was time to bid adieu to Patna and move on to another city. This time, it was Ranchi.

6. Ranchi (1972 - 1974)

Father was promoted as the District Development Officer in United Bank, and hence, we decided to move to Ranchi after spending only 6 months in Patna.

Ranchi was a beautiful city in those days with very good weather. Those days, it was just a city in Bihar. Now, it is the capital of the state of Jharkhand and the city of M.S. Dhoni.

The name Ranchi is derived from the previous name of the Oraon village at the same site - Archi. According to legend, after an altercation with a spirit, a farmer beat the spirit with his bamboo stove. The spirit shouted *archi, archi* and vanished. "Archi" became Rachi which subsequently became Ranchi!

Ranchi is also known as the city of waterfalls.

As we came into Ranchi, the first 2 things that any family looks for is accommodation and schooling.

For the first time, all four of us (brothers) got admitted to Bishop Westcott Boys School. The school was founded in 1927 by Rev. Westcott, and it is one of the oldest schools in the Eastern part of India. It is located on the banks of Subarnekha river in Namkum. It is also close to the Namkum Railway station. The school building also served as the makeshift hospital during the 2nd world war. A lot of students from Nepal and South Asian countries study in this school. In our times, there were a lot of Chinese students as well. It has about 1800 students including day scholars and boarders.

The school was very far from the place we used to stay in Bariautu. It was almost 20 km, and we used to travel on a school bus. It used to take us almost one hour to reach the school.

Bariatu was a kind of a desolate place during those times. It had a lot of tribal or Adivasi people living in this area. It also had a few huge bungalows built by retired people.

We had rented one such bungalow.

This was a huge double storeyed bungalow, and we used to stay on the first floor. It was more than 2000 sqft. It had big rooms including a drawing room, a dining room, 3 bedrooms and a huge veranda. The landlady, a Bengali, used to stay on the ground floor. She lived alone. Her husband was a very big official in Tata Steel. He maybe was a General Manager or MD. I would not remember now. I did see her husband's photograph with Pandit Nehru in their drawing room. It was a beautiful house, and the lady maintained it likewise. She was a sophisticated lady with a rich taste.

In front of the house, there was a huge lawn with different kind of flowers. Behind the house, there was a huge space as well with 2 to 3 garages and a servants' quarters.

By virtue of his promotion, father got his first official car. It was an Ambassador. For many years, we would travel in the Ambassador car to far-flung places in Bihar and Orissa. Our first driver was Kali who again was an Adivasi. He was a great skilled driver who became a family member over the period of 2 to 3 years. He became the man Friday for us.

When Father used to go out of the town, Kali would stay with us with his *bhojali* to keep an eye and act as the bodyguard, so to say.

The maids were also Adivasis. They were very cheerful and hardworking. They would laugh loudly, and they were very clean. It was amazing to see how open and modern they were. They would talk freely about sex even with us and have a great laugh about it. We also never took offence. That is how those days were. Kali would also have a fling with this maid, and he would also talk about it with us! At the same time, they were very courteous, dutiful and loyal. If required, they would lay down their lives for their masters.

Today, we cannot imagine such open discussions.

This is the time we had one full-time maid who joined our house. She was Mary, a devout Christian. Her husband had died, and she needed to work to sustain herself. She was an efficient worker always dressed in crisp white clothes. She was dark, beautiful and elegant. She was with us for a few years. I do not remember as to when she exactly quit and went on her way

However, the area around us was desolate, and there were a very few bungalows around our house. By the time dusk set in and darkness fell during the winter, it became quite eerie.

There was another bungalow nearby where a Bengali couple used to stay, and we would frequent their house.

The school was different from the schools we had attended in Agra. Those days, the school was not doing so well, and the standards had fallen. But, it was still one of the best schools in Ranchi. There were a lot of boarders.

I remember that after lunchtime, all students would assemble in the huge courtyard. The prefects (senior students) would make a count to see if anyone was missing!

There were a lot of Chinese students who used to be boarders. They were not good students and used to bully us – the day scholars.

We also had the Vice Principal who was from Uganda. He was an ugly looking man who was notorious for his cane. He used to hide this cane in his trousers! And, he would use the cane very often.

The school had great facilities for games and all my brothers used to participate in Cricket and hockey. I was still small, and I was slowly making my way into these games. But, one game which caught my attention was **marbles or** "*Kanchhas*" **as we used to say. They were** of different colours, and there was one big white marble which was used to hit other marbles. In my recess, we would play this game every day. Depending on how skilful I was, I would either win a lot of marbles from others, or I would lose them. We also had a jar where we all kept our marbles. We would count it every day to see that none was missing!

There were many fights happened between students, especially, between classes 9 and 11 students. In those days, there were no board exams at class 10. It was senior Cambridge, and board exam was at class XI.

My eldest brother passed out from this school. His batch was the last to appear in senior Cambridge exam. Post that year it was changed to class X.

In one instance, there was a huge fist-fight between Mahendru, a class IX student, and some Jhunjhunwala who was a lanky class XI student. The fight became ugly, and the senior student was beaten square. He started bleeding. I would not remember the aftermath of this incident. However, the fights would continue.

Once, we were supposed to go to Calcutta in our Ambassador car immediately after our school closed for summer holidays. Our Dadu (grandfather) had come as well, and he was also supposed to travel back with us. We were excited. We changed our school uniform and waited for our parents to come. The car arrived, and we hopped into the car for our ride to Calcutta. However, after travelling for a few kilometres, the car developed a snag, and we could not go further. According to Mother, it was pre-planned by father as he never wanted to go. We were very disappointed not by the fact that we did not go to Calcutta, but because we could not do so by car. We had food outside and came back home.

We made many trips, and some were quite long in our Ambassador car. Today, it is surprising that how many of us fitted in the car. If we look back, it seems impossible. In our ride to Calcutta, we were eight of us including Kali, our driver. This was considered normal. However, if we had visitors like uncles and aunts, there would be 12 to 13 of us, and we would all fit in the same car! I still remember that my Mejda and I had to sit on the floor of the car! We would also see 15 to 16 people being fitted in other cars during those times. In these cases, Kali would sit a little diagonally in the driver's seat occupying as little space as possible, and he could drive for hours together.

My *Mejo Jethu* (uncle) visited us in Ranchi. There would be a lot of relatives visiting us during this stint, and we would go to many places around Ranchi. Our Choto Pisi (aunt) and our Mamas from Calcutta (uncles and aunts) would visit as well.

Jethu wanted to go to Gaya to do the "*Pindadan*"- It is a practice to honour the deceased ancestors, and he wanted to do for our Grandfather (paternal). Gaya is a holy city besides the Falgu river. We have not been there, and our parents had accompanied Jethu to the holy site.

Subsequently, our *Choto Pisha* and *Pisi* would come with their entire family and visited us. They had 4 children - 3 sons and one daughter. They stayed in a place called Bally which is in the suburbs of Calcutta. It was again great fun for us since the house was full. However, their family created a lot of nuisance in the house, and especially, in the washrooms. They were not used to the western commode, and they broke it! Maybe they attempted to stand on the same. The entire house became dirty. However, nothing could be said since they were family. They had a great time visiting Ranchi.

When we visited Calcutta, apart from visiting our *Mamabari* (maternal uncle), we would also visit our *Pishibari* (paternal aunt's place). They had their own house in Bally (not to be confused with Bali in Indonesia). This is a suburb outside Kolkata. Pisha (uncle) had his own double-storeyed house. He was a very influential person there. He had helped set up the school there. He used to work in the United Bank of India (same bank as my father). He was in the inspection department and used to tour a lot. He saved a lot of money from touring allowance by staying in the bank premises. He would sleep on the benches inside the Bank and save on the hotel cost. But, my *Pishima* (aunt) used to spend a lot of money, and she would buy 20 sarees at one go!

When we used to go there, we did not like it very much since their house was dirty. We had to bath in the "*pukur*" (water pond) which was very exciting though we did not know how to swim. All my cousins were very good swimmers. We had nothing much to do there as well. In fact, we liked our own house and our own place where we were free to do anything within a few ground rules set by Father.

While *Pisha* earned a lot of money, his sons and daughter (except the youngest son) were not very interested in studying.

Our stay got truncated in Bariatu for 2 reasons. (1) The area was very desolate and far off from the main city and our school. (2) Maybe, the landlady was not used to all kinds of *tamasha* happening in the house. She was a peace-loving and sophisticated lady.

We decided to move to another house in Burdwan Compound which was near Lalpur Chowk in the heart of the city.

This was again a house which was divided into 4 parts. We were on the ground floor, and the best part of the house was a room on top of the garage. This is the room where we 4 brothers would spend a lot of time, and it was our favourite place.

Then, our Mama, Mami and our cousins also came and visited us.

We went on trips with them, and that is the time we were huddled in one car and visited the falls and many places of interest for the tourists. As we know, Ranchi is the city of waterfalls. We visited all the waterfalls, each of them was beautiful and magnificent. I have never been back to Ranchi after that, and I do not know as to how it looks now.

Johna Falls - It is located about 45 km from Ranchi.

Dassam Falls is about 34 km from Ranchi. But, the best of the lot is Hundru Falls. The waterfalls has a height of 320 feet.

We also went to Tagore Hills. It is a scenic location. You can see the sunrise and sunset from the hilltop. It was also the ashram of Rabindranath's elder brother Jyotindranath Tagore.

I still remember that there is a government tourist lodge and restaurant. We used to have lunch over there which was a simple dish of chicken and rice. After lunch was over, I remember having washed my hands and then wiping the same on the curtains! Our rustiness was again evident to our Uncles who used to talk about this incident for a long time.

We decide to visit, along with our Uncles, a place called Rajrappa which was the abode of the famous *Chinnamastak* temple or the headless deity. The self-decapitated goddess holds her own severed head in one hand and a scimitar in another. Jets of blood sprout out of her bleeding neck and is drunk by her severed head and two attendants. It is a union of a *Bhairavinadi* (female coming from top) and meeting *Nada* (male). This deity is considered to be very *jagrut,* and many people from far off places come and visit the place.

Back in Ranchi, we would dine out with them. Ranchi was very famous for its Chinese restaurants, and there were many of them.

In one funny incident, our uncles and aunts, along with our parents, went to watch a movie. It was a Bengali movie called "Sanyasi Raja", and we watched it in one of the premiere movie houses. This movie house had 2 halls. It was something akin to the multiplex. The driver, Kali, was asked to bring the tickets for the night show. So, after dinner, they all went to watch the movie. Alas, the tickets which were bought were for the evening show, and the movie had been over! In the interim, Kali entered another show in the same house watching a Hindi movie. He was untraceable, and the car was locked. Those days, there was no mobile where you could be contacted. It was late in the night, and there was no transport available as well. Seeing no other alternative, they had to walk back the entire distance back home. They were all cursing Kali. But, it was their fault as well as they did not check the movie tickets which we normally do.

Another funny incident involving my cousin Joy and I could have become a little dangerous.

We were playing *chor-police.* This was a game where some people would hide anywhere in the house, and some people would find them. In one instance, our team was supposed to hide. All of us hid in different places. We asked Joy to hide in a very big trunk which we had kept in the room over the garage. This was huge trunk which was used during the transfers. It could easily accommodate one person comfortably. He was smaller than me, and hence he hid comfortably in the trunk.

Everyone was found, but he could not be traced. Finally, after some time when everyone came upon me including my Aunt, I pointed them to the trunk. Joy came out of the trunk. He was a little out of breath, and if he had stayed in the trunk further, it would have been really bad. I was obviously rebuked for doing something very stupid, and I agreed!

Our landlord had 2 daughters in their house. They were much older to us. One of them was in University, and the other one was in College. However, they were tomboyish, and they would mix with us. Once, they wanted my Mejda and me to be like girls. They dressed us up like girls with frocks, lipstick and hairdo! We had this photograph for a long time. I do not know whether it is still there.

Right opposite to our house was a garden with litchi trees. One day, both of them came to our house and proposed that we should climb over the compound of the garden when the guard was asleep and climb the tree to get the litchis. It is just not that we would go, they accompanied as well. All of us, including the four of us and the two sisters, climbed to the other side and got the litchis!

I had a bank as did many children in those days, and I had saved quite a lot of money. These sisters influenced me to break the bank and have a party! Later on, I got rebuked from my mother for having spent all my savings.

Such were these two sisters - beautiful, but naughty

and fun loving. I am sure they have become old now and must have children and grandchildren as well.

In the same building, there was another neighbour who stayed, and they had a daughter who was younger to me. Somehow, she would call my mother "*Sasuli*" in her childish voice which was meant to be "*Sasuri* or *Saans*" which meant mother- in – law! She wanted to get married to me! Such is the innocence of childhood, and my mother would also indulge her.

Father had a touring job. Mother would accompany him most of the times. If we had holidays, we would accompany them a well. If none of our brothers went due to school, I would be the one to go always.

We visited many places not only during his tours but also generally.

We went to Jhumri Tillayya. This was the birthplace of my three brothers. The Pandit family were still there. The elder son had become a doctor, the youngest son (Shyamal da) had joined United Bank of India, and was in Ranchi. Their daughter was studying in Patna.

My elder brother was called "Tilu" by them since he was born in Jhumri Tillayya!

Jhumri Tilliya is located in the Kodarma district and is currently a part of Jharkhand. It was then a major mica mining centre. Huge mansions were built by the businessmen here, and it was not uncommon to see a Mercedes or a Porsche car those days. The city once boasted of the most number of phone connections in India and most phone calls made in India! Most of the mica was exported to the USSR. With the dissolution of USSR and the discovery of a synthetic for mica, mica mining activity declined.

The location became famous in the 1950s owing to its connection with the radio channels. Radio Ceylon and Vividh Bharti (a national radio service of All India Radio). At a time when numerous TV channels and FM radio stations were yet to come to India, the radio shows were a national phenomenon. The largest number of requests for film songs came from this place - Jhumri Tillayya. Because of a large number of song requests and the town's unusual name, many listeners used to doubt its existence.

Even today, when I tell my wife of this, she does not believe it to be true!

We would also listen to a very famous song show named "*Binaca/Cibaca Geet Mala*" by Radio Ceylon which used to be hosted by Ameen Sayani. This was first started in 1952 and continued till 1988. It then shifted to Vivid Bharti service of all India Road where it ran till 1994. We used to look forward to this. This was a weekly affair on Wednesday for an hour. This was the collection of the 20 most popular Hindi Songs for the week based on votes by the Indian listeners based on requests made by them.

The show was extremely popular not only because of the songs but due to the voice of Ameen Sayani and the way he used to conduct the show. In fact, the show as legendary. Ameen Sayani is a cult figure as far as Radio announcers are concerned, and many have tried to imitate his style over a period of time. His now famous style of addressing the crowd or audience with *Bhaiyyo* and *Behno* is something which is etched in everybody's heart.

Another city frequented by us with Father was Giridih. This was also under his area, and he had to visit this place as well.

We also went along with him and stayed in the house of Kalyan Jethu (uncle) who had a very big double-storeyed house. His mica business was flourishing, and the mica processing was done on the same premises. He had three sons and two daughters. The first 2 brothers and the eldest daughter were elder to my dada (brother), and the youngest son was the same age as me, and the youngest daughter was the same age as my Sejda (brother elder to me).

Jethima (aunt) was a very enterprising and a lady of great work ethic. She would not only take care of the entire household, but she would also advise Jethu (uncle) on business matters, and she was very culturally inclined. Once, we had gone after Durga Pujas, and during that time, there was a full-fledged practice going on for a drama. Jethi (aunt) was the director. Those days, the para (colony) would organise their own indigenous dance and dramas which were directed and choreographed by them, and the participants were also from the para. No external help was taken.

Many years later, this bond between the two families would further get strengthened when my eldest brother's marriage was fixed with their youngest daughter, Sujata.

I will take a pause to talk a little about Giridih now.

As the name suggests, it is the land of hills and hillocks. It was rich in coal, and during those times, the town boomed due to the mica industry which was exported mainly to Japan. Many famous personalities spent some time here.

In the British period, this entire Chotanagpur area including Kodarma, Giridih, Hazaribagh was called "Paschim" or "West" by the Bengalis and many of the *Zamindars.* Scholars and poets would go and spend some time there because of the very pleasant and cool climate in these areas. People also visit these places to recuperate after an illness.

Sir Jagdish Chandra Bose spent his last days here, and he died here.

Jnan Chandra Ghosh was a scientist and the first director of IIT Kharagpur and the Vice Chancellor of Calcutta University. He also spent time, and so did Rabindranath Tagore. The house in which he resided, Dwarika Bhawan, still exists in Giridih.

Satyajit Ray, the great filmmaker from Bengal and the recipient of an Oscar, spent his childhood here. It is here that he sketched his fictional character (appearing in a series of science fiction books) scientist Professor Shanku while residing here on the banks of river Usri. In fact, it is said that Satyajit Ray wanted to make a science fiction film based on one of his science fiction stories. It was later made by Steven Spielberg "E.T." It is said to be loosely based on one of his science fiction stories from where it is supposed to be inspired.

We would also visit Hazaribagh which is also now part of Jharkhand. The distance from Ranchi to Hazaribagh is about 100 km, and it would take around 3 hours or more during those days.

We would travel in our Ambassador driven by Kali. The car would traverse between steep Ghats. They used to zigzag so much that they were called "*Jilebi Ghats.*" It was always prudent to drive during the daytime. But, on a few occasions, we would travel during the night time. The trucks would be travelling as well, and they used to drive dangerously. One had to cope with the Ghats as well as these big trucks or "Giants" as my mother would call them. She used to be very scared of them. All around the Ghats were dense forests. These used to be infested with wild animals and bandits. Hence, one would avoid driving in the night.

Hazaribagh is a beautiful city with a nice cool climate. It is a famous health resort, and it also has a wildlife sanctuary.

In ancient times, the district was covered by inaccessible forests inhabited by tribes who remained independent.

During British rule, one had to go first go to Giridih, and then, travel in a vehicle called push- push which was manually pushed by men to Hazaribagh. It was pushed over the hilly tracts. It was an exciting journey across rivers and through dense forests infested with bandits and wild animals. Rabindranath Tagore travelled once like this in 1885.

During British time, there was an army cantonment, and many Englishmen settled here. They built a large Bungalow like houses with sloping roofs. Most of them left after Indian independence. A century ago, it was common for tigers and leopards to prey upon livestock in the outskirts of the town. As there were wild animals, hunting was very popular here, and there are many tales of hunting which one can hear.

Hazaribagh central jail housed many leaders of the Indian freedom movement including Dr. Rajendra Prasad and the famous Jayaprakash Narayan. His escape with 52 dhotis and help from inmates is part of folklore in this part of India. It is one of the legends of the Indian independence movement.

A small but effective Bengali Community settled at Hazaribagh in the 19th century when the area was under Bengal Presidency, and the British were looking for English educated people.

I will go to some other places which we visited after a few small incidents in our lives during our stay in Ranchi.

We were a middle class and an extremely happy family. We used to be happy with very small things in our lives. Since we were a big family, we also learned to share with each other whatever limited resources or things which we had. Our biggest strength was 'us.'

Shyamalda (youngest son of Pandit uncle) who finds mention in the earlier part, was posted in Ranchi while working in United Bank of India; the same bank where my father worked.

He was short, muscular and had a big moustache. He used to travel on a big bike and had long hair. When he used to come to our house in the bike, and people in the neighbourhood used to think that he was kind of a "*mastan*" or a "*Goonda!*"

He would come and stay with us.

He once took us to a cricket match between two banks, and he was playing as a wicketkeeper. The one thing I would remember was when he was batting, he smashed the ball, literally in an overhead smash style more in the tennis or badminton style, and the ball sailed for a six!

When I watch IPL these days, I can see some similarity!

He had immense strength and had a big heart.

He was always around whenever the family needed him, and he became part of the family.

During the Diwali, we would go and buy crackers. As the resources were limited, the crackers which were bought were also not much. However, we used to be super excited. Once we would get back home, the entire crackers would be distributed equally between the four brothers and each would take away his share. It so happened that my brothers would burst those crackers very fast and they would then lay their hands on my share! It would generally happen with most things.

During this time, there were 2 incidents which were sort of related to each other. At least that is what my mother used to believe.

I remember that my father had gone out for a week's training to Bombay (now Mumbai). At that time, Anandamoyee Ma had come to Ranchi. My mother was God-fearing and spiritual, but she was not rigid. She had taken me to the Ashram of Ma in Ranchi.

Anandmoyee Ma was born in 1896 in Bangladesh. She was a Bengali Spiritual leader who gave her simple discourses in Bengali or precisely "Bangal" language. Precognition, faith healing and miracles were attributed to her by her followers.

I would remember that both of us were taken to her presence and both of us were fortunate to have that opportunity. "Ma" blessed Mother and gave her some discourse. My mother was so impressed that she wanted to take "*Diksha*" or become a disciple. She spoke to Father the same day and took his permission which he readily granted. The next day, mother took the *dikshha* directly from Anandmoyee Ma. She was probably one her few followers who would take the *dikshha* directly from her.

During all this time, I was suffering from acute pain in the abdomen. There was a burning sensation while I used to urinate and I used to do that frequently. It was accompanied by vomiting and fever.

Immediately after my mother took her *dikshha*, I was diagnosed with acute Nephritis which is due to the inflammation of the kidneys. If not diagnosed and treated in time, it can lead to kidney failure.

I was very sickly during my childhood, and I used to suffer a lot. Hence, my parents were over-protective of me.

The fact that this disease was immediately diagnosed after my mother's *dikshha* strengthened my mother's belief in Anandmoyee Ma.

After my mother passed away, we took her remains to Hardwar and put the remains in the Ganges and also visited Kankhal which is an Ashram of Anandmoyee Ma.

After I was diagnosed with Nephritis, it was considered to be very serious. I was advised complete bed rest. I could not have any spicy item. Food was supposed to be boiled. I also could not take salt in my food and had to take a lot of fluids.

So, I was on this diet for 3 months without any spice and salt! Just imagine. Everything was without any taste. I used to like chicken. My mother would prepare chicken which used to be boiled and without salt.

Throughout this period, my mother was always at my side. She would be awake the whole night looking after me. The next day would be hectic for her since she would have to look after the whole family though there were maids and servants with us.

Today, while she is not there, I miss her so much, and I feel her absence very much. It brings tears to my eyes while I write this. I was always her favourite.

I finally recovered fully from this dreaded disease.

There was one place which was very famous in Ranchi. It was Firayalal at the heart of the city. It was the only departmental store for clothing and other things. It was only one of its kind. Firayalal means, "one-stop" for all requirements of the family. This is a landmark in Ranchi and the oldest shopping complex in eastern India. We used to frequent that place very often. Our attraction was the vanilla ice-cream cone which was available in the coffee and ice cream shop in front of the store. This ice cream cone was famously known as "softie." We used to love having softies there. I am told that this store is still there, and so are the softies. But, it does not hold that attraction anymore. I understand that since there is so much to choose now amongst both Indian and foreign ice cream brands. But to us, we have loving memories of "softie."

I must mention 2 more trips which we made during our stay in Ranchi. One was Netarhat, and the other was Rahgirh.

Netarhat was about 145 km from Ranchi in Chotanagpur plateau, and it is a scenic getaway.

We had decided to go on a bus along with all local friends of the colony. We were all excited since we would be going on a bus. The idea was to go during early noon and reach there to catch the sunset. People usually went there to view the beautiful sunrise and the sunset. As luck would have it, the bus got delayed. We waited anxiously, but the bus never came. It was now evening, and the elders wanted to cancel the trip as the journey during the night could be risky. We would have to traverse within the Ghats and the jungles. But, we were adamant, and we wanted to go.

Finally, the bus arrived at about 8 pm in the night. We immediately boarded the bus and left for Netarhat. We had also taken our gramophone along with us, and we started hearing songs on the way. It was pitch dark as the bus made its way through the winding roads in the jungles and Ghats, and everyone was a little jittery. It was also known that the jungles were infested with dacoits and I am sure that today nobody would have risked travelling in the night. But, we did. I guess the times were different, and we were not worried about anything. Today, we worry about each and everything, and even the smallest of things.

Finally, we arrived at the guest house at midnight. However, the guest house was closed. We started playing music loudly which woke up the caretaker!

All other inhabitants started complaining as well. We finally got our rooms, and we went off to sleep.

We could not obviously see the sunset. But, we were eager to see the sunrise. We woke up early in the morning, packed our breakfast and boarded the bus which took us to the viewpoint. It was cold and chilly, and the viewpoint had many tourists. We finally saw the sun coming out with its magnificent splendour. It was really beautiful and was worth the wait. Later on, we would see sunrise and sunset from many places, but I would always remember Netarhat as the first place.

We ate out breakfast of boiled eggs and bread and returned to the guest house. After having lunch, we made our way back to Ranchi.

It was truly an adventurous trip.

We would also make a trip to Rajgirh.

Rajgirh was originally known as Girival in Nalanda district. This was the first capital of the Kingdom of Magadha, a state that would eventually evolve into the Mauryan Empire.

I liked 2 things about Rajgirh. The first one is the ropeway, and the second one is the hot springs.

The ropeway is the oldest in the country. It is a single person ropeway - that is only one person per seat. The ropeway runs to the top of the Ratnagiri Hill. It leads to the Vishwa Shanti Stupa of Buddha.

The ropeway is not only single, but you got to get on the ropeway at the top while it is moving!

Since I was small, my father did not allow me to sit in a single ropeway, and I had to sit with my father. That was another challenge. But, we managed to get into one. The journey upwards was pretty steep. My father asked me as to what I will do in case the ropeway stopped. I answered innocently that I would jump!

As luck would have it, the ropeway suddenly stopped due to a power cut. Our ropeway was perilously close to the hilltop. But, as I mentioned earlier, we were not afraid or scared, and we started chatting. From where we were, we could see that we were at a huge height from the ground and there was no way we could do anything if the power was not restored. I am not even sure whether the authorities had any power back-up in those days.

We remained suspended for a long time. All my brothers and my mother too were in different seats of the ropeway. I am sure if it was today, each one of us would have panicked, and all hell would have broken loose.

Nothing of that sort happened. The power was restored, and the ropeway restarted. We finally reached the hilltop. We saw the *Shanti Stupa,* and we were there for some time.

It was now time to go down the hill, and it was a bigger challenge. One not only had to board the ropeway in the running but also time our jump at the same time - father and son to coordinate the same!

We did manage to do it and boarded the ropeway for our downward journey. Fortunately, there were no further incidents.

We then proceeded to the Makhdum Kund, a hot spring adjacent to Vipula hills. The place is named after a Muslim saint- Makhdum Saheb. It is said that the hot spring has medicinal values, and having a bath can cure you of many diseases. We also had a bath there, and finally returned to Ranchi.

If one were in Ranchi, how can one overlook Jamshedpur? It is the steel city built by Jamshedji.

Father had planned a trip there. It was an official one, and we also went. Jamshedpur was a beautiful township, especially the TISCO colony which was really beautiful. I do not know why, but we had stayed in TISCO colony in one of the Bungalows of a senior officer. This was the first time we were staying in a bungalow which was air-conditioned. The bungalow was modern and sophisticated, and we all were very excited to stay in such a bungalow.

We also saw Jubilee Park, a beautiful park which had a layered park and beautiful flowers. It also had many fountains which would have different colours in the evening. It was and is a beautiful park.

Our stay in Ranchi was coming to an end. My father, as usual, got transferred again to Patna to the Regional Office! We were set to move again. My *Dada* (big brother) had appeared for Senior Cambridge, (class XI) and had also appeared for Joint entrance. While he got through, he did not get the stream of his choice. He decided to join the Science College in Patna and take another attempt. My second brother was in class X and was due to appear in board exams. Hence, he decided to stay back in Ranchi in the hostel until his board exams.

There was a tradition in our family that one would get the first wristwatch after passing class X. None of us had any before class X! It would appear so ridiculous today when children not only have expensive watches but mobiles and tabs as well.

So, *Dada* was the first to get a watch from father. It was an HMT watch. This practice continued till I also got my HMT watch on passing my ICSE exam. However, before this, Dada was given a Seiko watch by my *Choto Mama* when he was younger. He was the privileged one amongst us!

It was time to leave Ranchi, and move to Patna for the 2nd time.

While we were leaving, my mother had told Mejda (2nd brother) who was now in the hostel to come to Namkum station which was just beside the school so that she could see him.

However, Mejda was so busy with his hockey that he forgot to come to the station. My mother was waiting on the steps of the train as it passed the Namkum station eager to catch a glimpse of her son. But, she was disappointed since Mejda had forgotten all about it, and was busy with his game of cricket. He became so involved in his game that his studies suffered. My mother had to come back shortly to Ranchi and rent a small house so that Mejda could stay in the house and study for the board exams!

We once again had to leave behind our friends we made during our stay in Ranchi. It was a beautiful city, and we felt sad about leaving it. We had to bid adieu to Kali (our driver) who had become part of our family. However, we would be lucky to get another equally good driver in Bahadur in Patna.

7. Patna (1974-1976)

Patna is the capital of the state of Bihar and a very ancient city. It was known by the name of Pataliputra and was the capital city of Magadha. Many scholars and astrologers belonged to this city including Aryabhata, Chanakya and Kalidas.

Patna is situated on the banks of the river Ganga.

We took a house in Rajendra Nagar. It was a double-storeyed house. This house belonged to the Ex-Vice Chancellor of the Patna University. It was a huge house. We used to stay on the first floor. In the ground floor, a Punjabi family used to stay (Kapoor). They had one son who was in college and two really beautiful girls. The elder sister was probably in class XI or class XII. The 2nd sister was probably in class VII or VIII. They were real beauties. I still remember once when we were sitting on the steps of the house after we had finished our game of cricket. Suddenly, the elder sister came and asked Sejda (brother) whether "aunty" (Mother) was there in the house. Sejda started stammering and could not speak properly. He was stunned not only by the sudden appearance but also by the beauty of the lady!

Rajendra Nagar is named after the country's first President Dr. Rajendra Prasad. It is a planned colony divided by numbered roads. In those days, it was a posh area to stay. It has several parks and playing fields where we used to play cricket.

I was admitted to a school which was in Rajendra Nagar - St Francis. It was a good school with very good teachers. If I remember correctly, it had mostly lady teachers. It was a co-ed school, and it was only a primary school. The principal of the school was Mrs. Raj who was a rather sophisticated lady. I enjoyed my stint in this school. It was a good school with good academics. There was a playground behind the school, and we used to play cricket there. By this time, I was also getting good in this game and was becoming sought after in the matches. I also remember that I participated in the school sports which would have the sack race, the spoon and marble race, memory game and running race. I also remember that I stood 2nd in the race, and that photograph is still there in our family album.

The teachers were so good that we also went to their houses. Our class teacher was a young lady - maybe 21 or 22. She once invited some of us to go to her house. She used to stay in the same colony.

I would just like to pause here. During those days, we were given a lot of freedom. We would go by ourselves to school, to play, to the teacher's house and to friend's place.

All these were not very near to our house. But, we were always given the freedom to be on our own, unlike today when parents accompany their grown-up children as well wherever they go!

Come to think of it, I was only 9 or 10 years old, and I would be on my own.

The children were mischievous as well. Since there were girls in our class, the boys would make a pass to the girls at that age. Just imagine!

They would make suggestive remarks which had a double meaning!

Another reason for attraction for this school was that they would show us Hindi movies once a month in the small auditorium which we had and. On many occasions, they would repeat the same movie! The most popular movies shown to us were "Namak Haram" and "Anand."

I have another funny incident which I remember. During Geography class, whenever the river Mediterranean was discussed, I had a great problem pronouncing the same. I could never do. My teacher would patiently try and make me pronounce it. However, I could not. The more I tried, more difficult it would be. Finally, after many such attempts, I was finally able to pronounce it, and it was a great relief for me.

Sejda (brother) and later on Mejda, after completing his board exams, got admitted in St. Sevrens School. It was not a particularly good school. Today, it is much better, and it is a larger school. Anyways, the schools in Patna were not as good as we were used to be. Dada (brother) got admitted to Patna Science College. However, he was more interested in Engineering and was getting prepared for the same.

We used to play a lot of games after our school, and it was ranging from Cricket, Gully Danda, *Chor-police*.

Obviously, after the games, we used to be famished. On many occasions, we would have *Kwality* ice creams. We used to get the orange stick at 15 paise which was amazing!

However, we would not have money to have snacks outside. But, there was a solution. However, it was not on a daily basis and not regularly.

During marriage seasons, we would see the "Baraat "coming to the bride's place. It was usually a large gathering. Taking advantage of that, we would mingle with the "Baraat" and enter the Bride's house! We would take care to comb our hair and wash our faces. In fact, the bride's household would think that we were part the bridegroom part, and they would put a garland across us! Nobody would notice us. We would drink cold drinks, have snacks like "*chanachur*" "*ladoos*", and then, before anybody would notice, we would slip out!

We did this on many occasions. It was adventurous, and we used to have a great laugh after that.

On a few occasions, since I was small, I would slip in the through the backside of the *shamiyana* where the food was being prepared. I would quickly sneak through and grab some food items, and sneak out. However, this was risky, and we did not take chances after a few attempts!

We were still not literate with Bengali. None of us was, except, probably, Dada (brother). He could read and write Bengali.

But, this is the time I started reading. It started with Hindi literature and Hindi fiction. I started with Munshi Premchand. Then, I gravitated towards Hindi fiction like Gulshan Nanda who used to write romantic novels. Many of his novels, later on, were made into Bollywood movies. I'm not sure if I was supposed to read those novels at that age, but I did.

Then, there were many spy thrillers in Hindi like Colonel Ranjit who was more like a James Bond character! Then, there were children's thrillers like Ram/Rahim which were teenage crime busters. We were all addicted to this genre.

At the same time, we started reading a lot of Indrajal Comics – Phantom, Mandrake, Panchatantra and heroes.

Then, there were English cartoons, and Tintin was among the most loved ones. Apart from Tintin, there was **Richie Rich, Asterix, Archie's** and Jughead, Obelix and many more war comics. Our entire childhood was filled up with these books and comics. I still feel that I should have probably kept those comics and books. They are available even today, but you have to shell out a bomb for that.

My reading habits started from a very young age, and I would become a vociferous reader of all kind of books in

English and mainly in Bengali. It would encompass literature, history, mythology, fiction and thrillers. Later on, my life, while I was still in school, I would read Leo Tolstoy- War and Peace and Anna Karenina, Somerset Maugham - of Human Bondage, Ayn Rand - Atlas Shrugged, William Shakespeare, Charles Dickens, and many more classics and at a very young age. I would love authors who wrote thrillers like James Headley Chase, Robert Ludlum, Jeffrey Archer, Agatha Christie, Harold Robins, Sidney Sheldon, Fedrick Forsyth, Enid Blyton and many others. I would look forward to the summer holidays when I would have books and comics to read. I could sit in one place and ready for 3 to 4 hours at a stretch. Then, I would take my bath, have lunch and go back to books.

On the newspaper side, it was always the *Statesman.* It was the only paper which would come to our house till we grew up and started taking other newspapers like the *Telegraph* and *Times of India. Statesman* is an English daily newspaper which was founded way back in 1875. It is owned by the Stateman Ltd and headquartered at Statesman House, Kolkata. The *Statesman* was characterised by its terse reporting style. It used to hold an independent, anti-establishment position. It vehemently opposed the emergency imposed by Mrs. Gandhi in 1975. To us, it was a drab kind of a newspaper. But, Father was a staunch statesman supporter, and we never had any newspaper apart from this. Now *Statesman* has lost ground to other newspapers like *Telegraph*, the *Times of India* and *Hindustan Times.* But, even now, it is the newspaper to be read for serious news reports, which are incisive, analytical articles and usage of a good standard of English.

On the English magazine side, father used to subscribe to *Illustrated Weekly*, which was a weekly newsmagazine publication in India. It started publication in 1880 as *Times of India Weekly Edition*. Later, it was renamed as *Illustrated Weekly of India* in 1923. It was considered to be an important English language publication in India for more than a century. The magazine was edited by people like A.S. Raman, Khushwant Singh and Pritish Nandy. Many young students, including us, would use it for regular reading and as a guide for honing English language skills in vernacular India.

Later on, there would be many sports magazines which would get introduced like *Sportsworld* and *Sporstar*. We would eagerly wait for the editions to come out and hog the magazines. It would cover international sporting events like the World Cup, the Olympics as well as the Cricket which was the unofficial national sport of India. Apart from that, it would cover tennis and Formula One Grand Prix as well. The magazines would also have posters of our favourite players, and these posters would be pasted in the doors/walls in our rooms.

Sportsworld is now a defunct magazine. It was started by Ananda Bazar Patrika, and Mansoor Ali Khan Pataudi was its first editor. It was sold to another sports magazine, Sportstar, which was a Hindu group publication from Madras.

Sporstar was founded in 1978 and was redesigned from

a magazine format to a tabloid format in 2006. However, we stopped reading and subscribing to these magazines once we started our families. I would not know why, but these magazines stopped coming to our house. While many of these would have become defunct, for some, their quality would have declined. Many of them would have become so expensive that we were not able to afford it. The Tintin series or the Asterix series, which cost a bomb nowadays, haven't reached our children. However, some of the movies made on these characters have created some amount of familiarity among today's children.

Our house in Rajendra Nagar was adjacent to the Moin Ul Haq stadium. In fact, we could see the stadium from our house. The stadium had a capacity of 25,000 people. It was initially named as Rajendra Nagar stadium. It was renamed in 1970 after the death of an icon, Moin- ul- Haque who was the General Secretary of the Indian Olympic Association.

We saw many cricket and football matches. The first cricket match we saw was the Ranji Trophy match between Bengal and Bihar. Bengal had Gopal Bose and Subrata Guha while Bihar had Ramesh Saxena and Daljit Singh. All of them were very talented players but were not be able to make it to the national team. Even if they made it, it was for one or two matches. The match was fiercely contested. However, the match ended in a draw. Those days, very few players from Bengal and Bihar would make it to the national team which was the hegemony of Bombay and Delhi.

We also witnessed the Santosh Trophy which is the national team championship between the states, and West Bengal has won the maximum number of times. Those days, it was mainly Bengal and Punjab. It was a delight to watch Surojit Sengupta the winger in the Bengal team who would sprint down the flank and lob the ball in the penalty area or would dart inside the penalty area himself. Then, there was the legendary Shyam Thapa who used to make the famous bicycle kick which would thunder into the goal post.

In the final, Bengal defeated Maharashtra by one goal.

We would often go to the stadium after our games, and just sit there.

Our greatest remembrance of the stadium is the drama which was based on the Indian war of Independence. This was enacted over a period of one month. One side of the stadium was reserved for the audience, and the entry was completely free. We would all go and watch. On one side of the stadium, the drama would unfold like the Indigo revolt, or the hanging of Bhagat Singh, or be the downfall of the Mughal Empire, or the freedom at midnight being enacted or the development of modern India.

It was a light and sound show along with acting on the stage - which was the entire stadium. I do not know how to describe this. But, surely, this was one of the most fascinating and impressive shows I have seen on such a large scale.

The memory is still very vivid when the Indigo revolt

used to be enacted, and the poor peasant would say, "*Dhan nayi boyega to khayega kya.*" (If we do not harvest the crop, what we will eat?)

The British soldier would reply in anglicised Hindi. "Dhan boyega to kora khayega, chabuk khayega." (If you do harvest, you will be caned!)

It was an absolute classic, and it seemed real.

This used to be organised by the state and the central governments. It was truly amazing!

The state government has now decided to demolish the stadium and build it afresh to make it suitable for national and international sporting events. The last international sporting event was a World Cup match between Zimbabwe and Kenya which was held in 1996. Since then, it has been in a dilapidated condition for the last two decades.

While we were in Patna in 1975, the inaugural One Day World Cup was played in England in the name of Prudential Cup. By this time, we were die-hard cricket lovers - all of us including our father. We would not miss the matches. Obviously, there was no television at that time, and we would listen to the live BBC commentary which would start in the afternoon.

India did not have much of an experience in One day cricket, and the side was led by Srinivas Venkat Raghavan. India's first match was against England who scored more than 330 runs in 60 overs. Those days, it was 60 over match compared to 50 overs which we have now. Dennis Amis scored a century.

In reply, India could only manage 132 for 3 in 60 overs! Can you imagine, one Sunil Gavaskar played for full 60 overs and scored only 32! This was a bizarre innings. No one and even Gavaskar could give any proper reason for having played that kind of an innings. India defeated East Africa in the next match by 10 wickets, but lost to New Zealand and Glen Turner, one of the best batsmen of New Zealand who scored a fine century to guide New Zealand to a victory.

India ended their World Cup campaign poorly. Finally, it was West Indies vs Australia in the finals, and it was a close match in which the Windies finally won. It also started the domination of the West Indies over cricket in the next 10 to 15 years. It led to the emergence of players like Viv Richards, Roy Fredricks, Gordon Greenridge and Alvin Kallicharan, led by the "Big cat" - Clive Lloyd. The fearsome quartet of pacemen in Andy Roberts, Michael Holding, Joel Garner and Colin Croft (or) Malcolm Marshall was a battery of superfast blowers who would pulverize batsmen across the globe. The Windies would win again in 1979, and their run would be stopped by Kapil's devils in 1983.

The year 1974–75 saw India winning its first World Cup in Hockey. Again, our source was the radio commentary that we used to hear on our dear Murphy radio. The world cup was held in Kula Lumpur, Malaysia, and India defeated its arch-rival Pakistan in the final by 2 goals to 1. The side was led by Ajitpal Singh and had many great names like Ashok Kumar who was the son of the legendary Dhyan Chand.

The radio commentary by the iconic Hindi commentator Jasdev Singh used to be so vibrant that we could actually imagine that we were watching the game. Jasdev Singh and Hindi commentary would go hand in hand. He would continue giving running commentary in the years to come for hockey in both Olympics as well as World Cup Hockey.

If Jasdev Singh was associated with radio commentary for Hockey, it was Sunil Doshi with cricket commentary. His description of the game and ball by ball commentary was really amazing. We grew up by hearing these iconic people providing radio commentary.

The journey of Patna would be incomplete if I do not talk about the great flood of Patna in 1975 and we would never forget. At least, I have not seen a flood of such magnitude and such force which can destroy both lives and property to such a large extent.

Bihar is India's most flood-prone state with 76% of the population in north Bihar living under the threat of recurring flood devastation.

It is all so vivid in my mind. We were six of us in the family at that point. It was a usual night, maybe a Saturday or Sunday in the last week of August. We were sleeping soundly with the only sound being the humming of the fan. Suddenly, we could hear an announcement which was distant. We woke up, and as we went towards the balcony. The announcement sounded clearer now.

It was basically warning the inhabitants of Patna of the

impending flood which was due to hit the city in the next 12 hours. By this time, everyone in the colony had awoken, and all the lights were on. We came to understand that the bandh near the Danapur Cantonment had broken due to which the water was going to enter the city. Water was also getting released from the dams built on river Son. This was to be the worst flood which would ever hit the city of Patna.

The anxiety and the related commotion had started. However, our family was chilled out. There was no reason to be anxious as we did not have much food or daily necessities. But, we did not make an attempt to go out and buy anything at that point in time. Maybe our parents did not realise the seriousness or the gravity of the issue. The lights of all the shops were lit. You could see the hustle and bustle.

Anyways, we went off to sleep. The next morning, mother and I went out to a local shop and brought some salt. I am sure we did not have many things besides salt only. It seems Mother thought we needed provisions only for a day! When we were coming back, we would see **water gusting through the** "*nallas.*" **It had great speed** though it had not spilt over to the roads. Now, we realised that the matter was serious, and we rushed towards our house. None of us had gone to school or college. By this time, the water was fast flooding the streets even though it had not reached great heights.

However, Dada had got his admission in Birla Institute of Technology, and he had to travel to Ranchi to get admitted. There was no option. He had to move out immediately with his bags and baggage, and make his way to the Railway station. I still have a vivid image of Dada (elder brother) carrying his suitcase on his head and wading his way through the waters. With the help of the army, he finally managed to reach the railway station.

Imagine, those days, there were no mobiles, and there was no way to keep connectivity. We would not get any news of him until he reached the station. Finally, he managed to reach the station, and catch the train to Ranchi. Fortunately, he had moved out in time, or else, he would have got stuck.

My father in the interim had asked the ground floor family, the Kapoors, to move to the 1st floor. They had started moving from early morning with clothes, valuable, and as much furniture they could move. Most importantly, they moved with a huge stock of food. It turned out to be great since we really did not have a stock of food. We had the pleasure of having Punjabi food with *Aloo parathas* and *Subji* and all Punjabi delicacies.

Imagine, great Punjabi food and the company of the beautiful ladies for so many days!

But on a serious note, this community feeling, where each and every one was trying to help each other is no more there, and the concept of community, para, neighbours are not there.

Very soon, the water was gushing in the streets at great speed, and the current was high. The entire 1st floor was flooded. Before we knew, the streets were flooded to the extent of 10 to 15 feet!

From our balcony, we could see our neighbours who were on the 1st floor. They had to move to the terrace. This was the condition of most of the people who were in a single-storeyed house and had nowhere else to go. A lot of people had moved to Gandhi Maidan, which was the highest location in Patna City. Our car and many other vehicles were moved to Gandhi Maidan.

Fortunately, there was enough water to sustain two families, and the food was more than adequate. There was a hissing sound of the water, and it was really scary. After the water had settled to 10 to 15 feet, it became calm except the splash here and there. We finally settled down and had a good delicious afternoon meal which was prepared by the ladies of the house – mainly by Kapoor Aunty and her daughters. It was delicious. After our meal, we settled for a game of cards where everyone participated.

In the afternoon, we had a good siesta. We brothers slept on the floor while the ladies were given beds to sleep in the bedroom, especially the Kapoor's as they were guests.

Things were really getting worse, and we could hear the radio saying that the entire city was submerged and there was a huge loss of life and property. The central and state governments were trying, on a war footing, to help out the people. We also heard that helicopters would soon be pressed into service for distribution of food.

We could see with our own eyes that the Sikh family across the street were struggling. But, credit to them, they were jovial and were always in a good mood trying to be in good spirits.

The day ended, we had our dinner, listened to the radio and went off to sleep. As usual, our "Murphy "radio was our companion. We would listen to *Binaca Geet Mala* and a very popular Hindi program- "*Hawa Mahal.*" We would also listen to songs on the gramophone.

The next day was no different. We were in no hurry to get up since there was no school, college or office to attend. We woke up and could hear the splashing of the water in the streets. We realized that we were marooned with water all around us. It was like the feeling of Robinson Crusoe in an island. However, we were not alone, and we had company.

We spent the entire day with a lot of fun with great "*adda*" session, playing cards and having a sumptuous lunch.

In the early evening, we could hear the buzz in the sky. The buzz was strong, and we rushed to the terrace.

There, we could see the helicopter hovering around the houses and dropping food and water. The chopper came just above our terrace, and we waved to them. We could actually see the pilot and another person very closely since they were close to the terrace. Then, they dropped a sack to our terrace. We were thrilled!

The sack contained packed food like *chura*, puffed rice, biscuits, candles, match boxes, *sattu* and many other items.

We did not need these things, but the thrill of getting it was great.

In the next few days, the choppers would make many rounds and drop food at our terrace. Each time, it would be an amazing feeling to see the helicopter from such a short range.

Everyone in the house, including all the ladies, would line up in the terrace. Now, in hindsight, it would seem that since the pilots saw some beautiful ladies in distress, they dropped more food at our terrace!

Finally, after 3 to 4 days, the water started subsiding. The pumps were used to flush out the water.

There was a bad stink all around, and the next fear was the outbreak of cholera.

Finally, the water totally subsided. All trees and plants were destroyed, and all vehicles were spoilt. Precious lives, documents and assets were all lost. Many people had developed depression as they had suffered losses. We were lucky. We were safe, and we survived without much difficulty. But, the memory of it is still alive. The Kapoors moved out and went to their ground floor which was in bad shape. They had to clean up the place which was quite a task. Most of their furniture was damaged. The Sikh family could also move down to the ground floor from the terrace

We were also sad because in these few days, we had really become one family, and we really had a good time.

The next day, army personnel arrived with doctors in the entire colony and started moving from house to house. They started inoculating each and every member in every house. The injection was a long one, and pretty painful. The pain remained for quite some time. But, kudos to the government for acting swiftly, and preventing the outbreak of any sort of epidemic.

Finally, everything settled down, and Patna was back to its usual self-having witnessed the worst ever flood in the history.

We had to move out of the house to another one in the same colony. This was in line with our tradition of changing one house in every city! This house was one building with multiple flats. This flat was good but not as big as the earlier one. It did not have too much of open space.

When we moved on to this house, we came to know that the landlord's son (Lalan Singh) was a dreaded mafia gang lord, and they stayed on the ground floor!

In fact, my mother had come to face to face with this person one day while she was getting down the stairs, and this person was extremely polite and greeted my mother as well.

It was also rumoured that there were many attempts on his life, and he had escaped many times. Once, he was in his sister's place when the assailants started shooting. While he escaped, his nephew fell to the bullets.

Once, while I came home from school, there was a huge crowd in front of the house and a posse of policemen.

Luck had finally run out for Lalan Singh, and he finally met his death – a violent one. He was torn to pieces by a bomb hurled at him from a close distance. Apparently, his head was blown off. They had brought his body to the house.

My mother had gone to their house to console his mother. The mother was a fiery lady. She picked up the sandal and apparently hit a very senior police officer for not being able to provide security to her son!

This was the ugly side of Patna with its gang rivalry based on caste.

Things settled down, and life was normal again. In fact, the youngest brother used to play cricket with us.

As usual, we used to watch a lot of movies. However, our stint in Patna coincided with the release of the iconic film in Bollywood – Sholay. It was released on 15th August 1975. This was a multi-carrier film with Amitabh Bachchan, Dharmendra, Jaya Bhaduri, Hema Malini, Sanjeev Kumar and newcomer Amjad Khan in the iconic role of "Gabbar Singh."

Initially, the movie did not have very good reviews. But, word of mouth led to the huge success. In every city, it was a silver or golden jubilee. Those days, there was no multiplex, and silver jubilee meant that it ran for 25 weeks, and golden jubilee meant it ran for 50 weeks.

We also saw the movie, and the dialogues became a part of our culture. Very soon, all of us were giving delivery of the now famous and cult dialogues like- "*Kitne aadmi the?*" or "*Sarkar ne humare upar kitne inam rakhe hain?* "or "*Thakur, yeh haat mujhe de.*"

We remembered all the dialogues of the movie and would remember each sequence of the movie. In fact, the dialogues became such a hit, that the entire film was released in a cassette. We bought that as well, and we listened to it regularly.

Gabbar Singh became a household name, and Amjad Khan made a grand entry to the Hindi film Industry.

Another movie which released around the same period and created ripples in the Bollywood Industry was the iconic "*Deewar.*" Released in 1975, the story was written by Salim Javed. *Deewar* is considered as a groundbreaking cinematic masterpiece. It was loosely based on the life of *Hazi mastan.* The acting and dialogue of this movie were its high points. The film had a significant impact on Indian cinema by cementing Amitabh Bachchan's popular image as the "angry young man.". This movie was a super hit, and I became a die-hard Bachchan fan. From here on, I would never miss his movie. Though, much later, in the late 1980's or early 1990's, he started picking up the wrong kind of movies. That was the time I also missed some of his movies which were really poor in both content and acting.

Another movie released in 1975 created news as well; though for different reasons. This movie was "Jay Santoshi

Ma," It was a religious movie based on the Goddess of satisfaction. This movie was made on shoestring budget and created a huge revenue. In most cities, it had a silver jubilee run. The film apparently made 5 Crores. The viewers often turned the cinema hall into a temporary temple by leaving their footwear outside at the door. They pelted flowers and coins at the screens and bowed reverently whenever the Goddess appeared! My mother was one of them who would become a staunch devout of Ma Santosh and started the puja after watching this movie.

The puja had to be done for 16 Fridays, and on each of this Friday, she would offer *Gur* and *Channa* to the Goddess. Once the Puja was over, the *Gur* and *Chana* would have to be given to the cows to be fed. On that day, all of us were prohibited to eat and touch sour things!

Finally, after 16 weeks, a grand puja will be done, and *Bhog* will be prepared. Children will be called to have the *Bhog* once the puja was done.

This movie created a whole mass of people who started worshipping Ma Santoshi. Currently, I do not see Ma Santoshi being worshipped.

Before I move further, I just wanted to comment on the prevalent style of those days.

Dada used to be very stylish, and he would embrace the styles of those days. We had bell-bottom pants. They used to flare out from the bottom of the calf, and the circumference was 18 inches in circumference at the bottom of each leg opening. The greater the circumference, greater the style.

All of us wanted to wear bell-bottoms. But, all of us were not allowed to wear. Dada, in fact, used to wear huge belts across the bell bottoms and colourful shirts along with high heel boots. One of the in-vogue cloth materials was *strechlon* trousers. These were also worn by Dada.

Those days and till about the late 80's, we used to get our clothes which were stitched by the tailors and readymade clothes were not in vogue. And we normally got new clothes only during Durga pujas.

Dada had got through both Joint entrance and BIT Ranchi. He had got through Shibpur Engineering College, but he was not getting a Mechanical stream which he wanted to pursue. He got this in BIT Mesra Ranchi, and he decided to move there. Those days, Engineering was a 5-year degree course.

Father had to take a loan to get his fees and expenses funded. Dada was my father's favourite son, though he would never give any indication of the same. But, we could realise it over the years.

Finally, the time had come for my Dada to leave the house for 5 years and go to the hostel. My mother was absolutely heartbroken, and so was my father (though he would not show it).

However, if one had to make a career, one had to go out. It was also time for us to move out of Patna.

Father had become a victim of office politics where the Regional Manager did not like him. The regional manager used to prefer another officer who was father's colleague and a Bihari. I am guilty of being provincial here. But, that was the core of the issue. My father had worked mostly in Bihar and UP, and he prided on the fact that he knew Bihar better than most people. However, he was told that he did not understand Bihar better than the person from Bihar.

Father got emotional and asked for transfer this time from HO to a city in his native state – Durgapur, Bengal.

It was time to pack our bags again and move to another city and State.

8. Durgapur (1976-1978)

Durgapur is an Industrial city being founded by Dr Bidhan Chandra Roy who was the first Chief Minister of West Bengal. It happens to be the 2nd most planned city in India after Chandigarh. It has many industries like Durgapur Steel Plant, Mining and Machinery Corporation, Philips Carbon, Graphite India and many others.

The city has been named after a former Zamindar, Durga Mohan Chattopadhyay

We first settled down in Sagarbhanga, a small colony in Durgapur. Our flat was very near to our Bodo Jethu's (Eldest Uncle's) house. Both Jethu and Jethima were alive and lived with their children and family. Theirs was a big family, and they had eleven children including 7 daughters and 4 sons. A full-fledged football team! Some of them were as old as my father.

Father had earlier organised a job for one of my cousins as a fitter in Philips Carbon Ltd during his initial stint in Durgapur. Initially, he was reluctant to do a labour kind of a job. However, reluctantly, he stuck on to the job and rose through the ranks.

Now, he was well settled, had become an officer and had a beautiful, well-furnished bungalow in the PCBL's own colony. It was such a beautiful campus with lovely gardens and a full-fledged ground where one could play football and cricket matches. We used to go there frequently, and we also played a few matches there.

Not all of them stayed together. They were spread across Durgapur, Ranchi and Kolkata. Jethima (aunty) was very active, and she was quite a lady even at that age. She loved to drink tea. She lived a healthy life till the age of 100, and she passed away only recently. She used to love my mother, and they would chat away for a long time.

I was admitted to St Michele's school which was located in BidhanNagar where we would shift later as per our tradition of changing our house once!

While we were in Sagarbhanga, we were getting ready to get admitted to schools. We used to play a lot of cricket, and we were becoming good at that. In fact, even at that age, I could bowl a slower one! It was great fun to see big guys getting bowled by me failing to read my slower one and moving their bat much earlier!

My other brothers were equally good.

While we had finished playing one evening, I was taking tips from one of my friends to sit for the entrance test in one of the schools. He told me that I should prepare myself with the life of Lord Clive. The only Clive I knew at that point in time was Clive Lloyd, and I was not aware of the British general Robert Clive who had defeated Siraj Ud Daulah!

Anyways, I got admitted to St Michael's school. At that time, it was a school which had classes till class VIII. This school was established in 1966, and it is a private Christian Missionary school. Now, it is a high school up to class X11 with almost 3000 students.

During that time, there was a playing field where we used to play cricket. But, it was not very good. Now, it has a huge football ground and a basketball court. It is one of the best schools in Durgapur. I was happy in this school and liked the school. It was very near to our house as well, and I used to walk there.

My brothers got admitted to Central School which was far off from our house. This was done so that in case of any further transfers, they could get admitted to these schools which were there almost everywhere and at any point in time. Hence, there would not be any year loss due to the transfer of parents.

Ideally, Father should have put me in Central school as well. But again, their extra care for me did not allow them to put me in a school which was so far off, and, according to them, I would not be able to withstand the travelling distance.

The frequent change of schools in the middle of the year due to transfers led to me losing almost 3 years!

Central schools or Kendriya Vidyalayas were set up to educate children of Indian Defence services personnel who are often posted in remote locations. With the army starting its own Army Public School, the service was extended but not restricted to all central government employees as well. It has about 1085 schools across India. A uniform curriculum is followed by these schools all over India. By providing a common syllabus and systematic education, the children do not face education disadvantages when their parents are transferred from one location to another.

As has been our practice to change one house in each city, we moved to another house in the colony of Bidhan Nagar which was one of the posh residential areas of Durgapur at that point in time. It was a clean and a new colony. It was also very close to my school.

One of our favourite pastimes on weekends was to watch movies in the ground near our house. Everyone use to carry newspapers/small tools (moras) and sit in the ground on either side of the screen and watch movies. It was good fun to watch movies under the sky while having tea and Jhalmuri. It was a family affair as well with all of us including Mother, who was a great movie buff as well.

Another great experience was watching jatras in the open air and there used to be many reputed groups who used to come and perform. For those who are not familiar with this concept, it is a popular folk form of Bengali theatre spread throughout most of Bengali speaking areas of the subcontinent including Bangladesh and the Indian states of West Bengal, Bihar, Orissa and Tripura. The word Jatra means journey or going. The origin of Jatra or musical theatre is credited to the rise of Shri Chaitanya's bhakti movement, where Chaitanya himself played

Rukmini in the performance of Rukmani Haran. Jatra performance would resemble the Nautanki of Uttar Pradesh, Tamasha of Maharashtra and Bhaval of Gujrat.

Jatras are usually epics which last for 3 to 4 hours preceded by a musical concert to draw an audience. The performances are dramatic and over the top in stark contrast to theatre or movies. These dramatic dialogues are interspersed with songs and dance routines as well. The songs are usually sung by the actors. The cast, earlier, used to be predominantly male who also play the female characters.

However, now female actors are found in Jatras.

The first Jatra, if I remember correctly, was Amrapali, and then, there were many more.

While we would go to the cinema halls to watch movies as well, it was not a regular affair since there were a few cinema halls. More importantly, there were not many movies which used to get released those days. Hence, the weekly "open air" movie shows were a great hit those days with us.

While we were in Durgapur, I remember I went with my parents for the first time to Shanti Niketan - the abode of the Kavi guru Rabindranath Tagore. At that time, 40 years ago, it was such a calm and peaceful place with a lot of greenery around and the famous Rabindra Bharati. While I still frequently go to Shantiniketan for its different environment and peace, it is not the same place as it used to be then. There were not many hotels during those days, and we had stayed in the Government Circuit house.

One fine morning, while Mother and I were having tea in the garden of the circuit house, we saw Samit Bhanja and Robi Ghosh. On enquiring, we realised that they had come with the other cast members for the famous Bengali movie Jano Aranya which also included Soumitra Chatterjee and Sharmila Tagore. I watched this movie much later in my life though.

Another exciting time in our lives used to be the Bijoy Sammelan which used to happen after Durga Pujas (Bijoy Dashami) and immediately after the immersion of Devi Durga. This was the time people met with each other. Younger people would touch the feet of elders and take their blessings. People of the same age would embrace each other in what we Bengalis call as Kola Koli.

The only thing which we hated was to touch the feet of many people apart from our parents. However, the incentive was that you used to get a lot of snacks like Misti (sweets) Nimki (snack) and Ghugni with minced meats. In every house, people used to prepare all this, and people used to visit each other's house. Like in any other house, our mother also used to prepare these stuffs.

However, not every visit was pleasant. Sometimes, if you had gone after a few days, you would be served with the same Ghugni which had probably become a little stale.

I remember one instance where we were served with not so good snacks, and we were supposed to eat it. Unlike today, there was no option of not eating since it was considered to be bad manners if you did not eat what was served to you.

My mother also looked at us and indicated that the Ghugni was not good. I went out with the Katori of Ghugni unnoticed from the drawing room, and silently disposed the Ghugni outside the veranda and came back after sometime. Taking a cue from me, my other brothers also disposed of their Ghugnis as well one after the other! It was done so well that no one noticed.

Whenever we used to go as a family to someone's house, we would eagerly wait for snacks and goodies to be served. We four brothers were not interested in anything else but the food. We would sit quietly in our place, and waited for snacks to be served. However, we would not make a move until Father first took a piece. This reminded me much later of the film Satte pe Satta where Amitabh Bachchan (eldest brother) would first take a plate and serve himself and then the other 6 brothers would literally attack the food.

However, we were not as uncivilised as them. But, the food used to disappear as fast as it disappeared in that film.

Once, we had gone to one of my father's friend's place, and Aunty had just served us plates full of snacks. She had gone inside to get tea for the adults. As soon as she went out of the room and Father had initiated the ritual of taking a piece out of the plate, we immediately and swiftly finished everything on the plates. By the time Aunty came back, all plates were empty. As she returned with tea, her eyes went wide, and she had to go back and get more helpings!

Those days, people used just to go and visit people without taking appointments. Nobody used to mind that. The regular flow of guests was always there in our house, and we also used to visit friends and relatives without any kind of formalities. Today, we cannot go unannounced to anyone's house, nor do we expect anybody to come to our house without prior information. It has become formal in stark contrast to the informal inter-personal relationships which were far warmer and cordial.

My school memories in Durgapur were restricted by the fact that it was in this school – class V that I first learned to read and write Bengali. We used to play a lot of cricket in the playground of the school. Now, I believe that the school is very big with a bigger playground.

For the first time, I participated in a Hindi drama. The story was loosely based on the early life of Kalidas, and as part of the script, I sang a Hindi song as well. Apparently, I had done a fantastic job, and my play was appreciated by all including teachers and parents.

My mother used to be the one who used to take care of all household activities including grocery and day to day buying of fruits, vegetables and fish. I used to accompany my mother in some of these sojourns, though I would never the like the smell of fishes.

This brings me to the topic of inflation seen through my eyes, and how inflation has increased over a period of time.

Usually, the day when you get the salary is supposed to be the happiest day for the person earning it and the family as well. However, this was the day which we used to dread. This day would inevitably lead to a fight between Father and Mother. Mother would say that she would not be able to manage the family on the basis of what father gave her, and father could not help it since he only had that amount. It led to arguments and bickering. That is how the day ended. Those days, salaries were not very good, and father had to support the education of four children including the engineering education of Dada which was expensive in those days. He also had to support Grandmother as well. I would assume that his salary was not more than 6 to 7 K. Obviously, he never had any kind of savings apart from his Provident Fund and a few life insurance policies against which he had taken the loan as well to fund Dada's education. He never compromised on education for any of his sons.

However, things were not costly as well. As I was saying, a Rohu fish would be around Rs. 10 a kg, Boal maach which is known as helicopter catfish or Wallago catfish was sold at Rs. 5 per Kg. Compare this with Rohu at 250 to 400 Rs per Kg or Catfish at 300 to 500 Rs per Kg!

Everything was cheap from cereals and vegetables to house rent. I still remember in 1980/81; we used to have 16 phuckas or panipuris at per rupee! How many do you get for a Rupee now? You will get the answer. Also, the needs were very simple. There were no TVs, Malls, electronic gadgets or fancy clothes. None of us took tuitions in our early school life which is very common nowadays. I first took tuition in class ten. It was the same with my brothers.

Our house rent in Ranchi was Rs. 500 in 1973 for a 2000 sq. feet house! Another aspect was that we used to get groceries through a khata system. This means that we used to buy stuff and pay all together next month. A book was maintained to make records. This was not a good practice, and it continued for a very long time. So was the case with medicines at a later stage. All in all, our resources were limited, and the needs were many. But, this did not deter us from having a very happy and contented childhood.

It was time to move again.

Our tenure in Durgapur was over, and from Bengal, it was time to move to Orissa. Father was now transferred to Bhubaneswar as the Regional Manager. It was a good career move for him, and it meant that we (especially me) had to find another school. We needed to find a new house and new friends. The funniest part was that we knew that we had to move again after some time.

9. Bhubaneswar (1978-1980)

Bhubaneswar, the land of temples, is the capital of Orissa. It is known as the land of temples since it is believed that it has more than 1 lakh temples! Along with Konark and Puri, it forms the Golden Triangle. It is a spiritual and a historical city. The modern city of Bhubaneswar was established in 1948, and it replaced Cuttack in 1949 as the state capital.

The name, Bhubaneswar, is derived from 'Tribhubaneswar' which means the Lord of the three worlds.

As is the case, we first moved to a moderate house in Kharvella Nagar which was close to the Railway station and the famous *Lingaraj* Temple. I will talk about the various temples and places of interest in greater details a little later.

Dada was still doing his Engineering degree. Mejda and Sejda had no issues in finding a school. Since they were in

Central school in Durgapur, they easily got admitted to Central School in Bhubaneswar. I had to wait for some time before I got admitted to DM School (Demonstration and Multipurpose school). It was a large school and an institute where budding teachers who were doing their B.Ed. would take training. They teach in the classes at this school to qualify as a teacher. I was admitted along with another student - Chinmay Tripathi whose father was also in a bank - Punjab National Bank.

The first day, when I was standing in the assembly line, I was asked from which school did I come from. When I said that I studied in St Michael's school in Durgapur, they thought it was a very funny name and started laughing. I did not understand the funny part, and I was a little depressed. I thought that this would be a difficult place to study.

However, this school turned out to be one of my best schools from the perspective of having a great time. I became involved in a lot of games like cricket and football, and I became pretty good at that. We also played basketball, kabaddi and chess as well. I made some very good friends like Chinmay, Sajal, Biswaranjan, Pradip, Satyakam, Amiya, Nibrit and Durani. I lost touch with them after we moved out of Bhubaneswar. However, after many years, thanks to Facebook, I connected with many of them again. In fact, I met Biswaranjan in Kolkata after 38 years. Chinmay was a close buddy since we would regularly return from school together in his cycle. At that point in time, he was average in studies, and I used to be amongst the top 3. Chinmay, today, is in the US. He did his Engineering in Computer science from IIT Kharagpur. Such is life. Even today, we are connected with each other.

Gradually, I became quite popular in my class. Not only was I good in studies, but I was also pretty good in all sports including cricket, football, basketball and hockey. Very soon, I became the captain of my class team, though Biswaranjan was always the class monitor. In those days, girls and boys used to sit separately. Though we used to speak to them, we never forged any close friendship with them. It is for this reason that I do not remember any of them.

We created our own sports club and bought a cricket bat, a ball and a football which were the property of the class. At the end of the day, one person had to carry it back home.

Every day, during lunchtime, we would play cricket. After school hours, we would stay back and play as well.

Chinmay was not good at cricket but was very enthusiastic about the game. I would show him how to have a proper stance, though he continued to have a very odd one. Slowly and gradually, he became okay in the game. We would play with other sections as well, and it would be very competitive.

Section B had Amiya Ray who was a splendid fast bowler as well as a very good batsman. He had had great timing and was a very aggressive batsman. Later on, after some years, Amiya was the first student of the school who represented Orissa in Ranji Trophy cricket and also played for East zone as well. He became an attacking batsman and switched over to bowling off-spin. I feel proud that I used to play alongside him. In fact, when trials were being held for the school team where all the senior boys were playing from class XI and class X11, it was only Amiya and I who were part of the trials, and we were from class VIII. Even Amiya did not get selected. I was kept as a reserve for the school team, and that was a great achievement.

Many years later, Shiv Sundar Das, who was junior to us by 3 years in the same school would represent the Indian Cricket team and would play as an opener in a few tests. We used to play football as well as Kabaddi. But, I was not very good at Kabaddi since I was not very tough. Sajal, however, was our master raider. I also remember Satyakam Patnaik, who studied in Section B. He also used to bowl fast, and I faced him a quite a number of times in our matches. He was also the son of a famous playback Oriya singer. Later on, he would also come into Banking Industry and work for Stan C in Kolkata when I was working with ABN AMRO Bank in the same city. However, both of us were not aware of the same. It was only a few days ago I realised that. Currently, Satyakam is in the Middle East.

Sejda and Mejda were also creating a name for themselves in the Central school for Cricket and hockey respectively. Sejda got selected for the school team and played in the Central school inter-state tournament.

Mejda was pretty good in hockey, and he was selected for the school team. He even went for the national trials for Central school. Those days, the Central school used to have a team of their own who used to play in the junior national hockey meet. However, he did not make it to the final cut of the Central school junior team.

We were playing a lot of sports and excelled in them as well.

My memories of the first house were restricted to 2 things. Every evening there used to be a *Jatra* about the Kalinga war. This is the war in which Emperor Ashoka had ruthlessly killed lakhs of people and defeated the Kalinga king. I would remember one Oriya dialogue from this *Jatra* which went like this, "Utkal sainani, Pokai kiri, khai kiri, soyee jao. Auo jete bela Asoka asibo, aame tar songe loribo."

This roughly meant, "Warriors of Kalinga, cook, eat and go to sleep. When King Ashoka would come, we will fight him!"

Emperor Ashoka never gave a chance, and he butchered them.

Dhauli, near Bhubaneswar, was the site of the Kalinga war (262–261 B.C.) in which the Mauryan Emperor invaded and annexed Kalinga. One of the most complete edicts dating between 272–238 B.C. remains carved in rock 8 km to the south-west of the modern city-Dhaulagiri.

The other memory was the close proximity to *Lingaraj* Temple.

Lingaraj temple is a Hindu temple, and it is among the lakhs of temples the city has. It is one of the oldest temples and a prominent landmark of the city. The temple represents quintessential Kalinga architecture. The temple is supposed to be built by the Kings from *Somavamsi* dynasty with later addition from the Ganga rulers. The temple complex has 50 other shrines and is enclosed by a large compound. The temple compound is not open to Non-Hindus. However, recently, the Supreme court has decreed that Non-Hindus can enter the temple.

Going by the tradition, we again shifted our house to the more posh area of the city. It was Shaheed Nagar which still is one of the better residential places. It was a large single-storeyed bungalow and had huge space in front which included a garage, a courtyard and a huge space at the back where one could grow vegetables. The house was really big, and it had a large dining room, drawing room and 2 very large bedrooms. Ma and Baba would be in one bedroom, whereas, the three of us (brothers) and Thakuma (Grandmother) would occupy the 2nd bedroom. The courtyard was so large that we could, and we used to play cricket. Our house was very near to the National Highway with Cuttack on one side and Goplapur on another side.

While we were in Sahidnagar, we forged a very good friendship with another Bengali family of Shome. Dr. Shome was associated with the Government Medical College in Cuttack and had a Bungalow in Cuttack as well. He would travel back to Bhubaneswar every weekend. They had a large double-storeyed house, again with a garage and a large courtyard. They had a large family. One daughter who was already married at that time, and he also had five sons.

The eldest brother was working with Orissa secretariat. We used to call him Manuda. The second brother was called Kanuda, and he was a lecturer in a college. The third brother was called Babluda who had left studies since he had some issues with his mental health. He was followed closely by Khokanda, who was not strong with studies but was very good in Cricket and hockey. The youngest son was Sainik who used to study in Central school and was a year older to me.

Sainik was good in studies and was extremely good in cricket and hockey. Those days, hockey was played a lot amongst school kids, and we were not different. We used to spend a lot of time at their house. In fact, during the summer holidays, we would have our breakfast and go to their house. Since it was hot and we could not go out, we used to play cards for hours, and Aunty would also join us. We would then go back to our house and have lunch. Again, in the evening, we would go back to their house.

There was a big playground in front of their house, and every evening, we would either play cricket or hockey. In fact, when we used to play hockey, all of us did not have hockey sticks, and we used to use cricket stumps as hockey sticks. Khokanda was so good that he could dribble with the cricket stump and score goals! Amiya would join us whenever we used to play cricket since he also used to stay in Sahidnagar. Sajal also used to come frequently to our house. At times, I would also go to Chinmay's house which was also near to our house, and we played cricket with him as well.

However, there was an unwritten rule in the house which we all adhered to. We had to come back home before sunset no matter where we were.

Since Uncle Shome had a bungalow in Cuttack, Sejda and I made a trip there along with Babluda, Khokanda and Sainik. It was for the first time that we saw 2 movies a day. I still remember that one of the movies was *Chacha Bhatija*.

We also made a family trip to Cuttack along with the Shome family and spent time there during Durga Pujas. Cuttack has a fair sprinkling of Bengalis, and Netaji had studied here in the famous Ravenshaw College. During the evenings, we would gather on the terrace. From there, we would watch the evening programme where many singers of repute from the Oriya Industry would sing. Satyakam's father was one of them. We used to have a great time.

Many years later, when I came back to Bhubaneswar as a married man with my wife and my parents, I made it a point to visit them. I recognised their house and took my wife as well. We met Shome Aunty. However, Shome Uncle had passed away. We could only meet Babluda who was still the same. Sainik was married and stayed in another flat. However, Shome Aunty did not talk about Khokanda. I still wonder why? Did he fall into the bad company? The visit kind of saddened me because a lot of things had changed.

Our house in Sahidnagar was very close to Dahuli, Khandigiri, Nandan Kanan, Cuttack and Puri. While Cuttack was at a distance of 30 minutes by road, Puri was at a distance of 45 minutes to one hour.

We would love to go to another place frequently. It was the Shanti Stupa in Dhauli about 7 to 8 Kms away from our place and on the way to Puri.

Shanti Stupa is located on Dhauli hills which are located on the banks of the river Daya. It is a hill with a vast opening space adjoining it. It has major edicts of Ashoka engraved on a mass of rock by the side of the road leading to the summit of the hill. As I mentioned earlier, Dhauli hill is presumed to be the area where the Kalinga war was fought. Ashoka had a special weakness for Dhauli where the battle was fought. The Daya river is said to have turned red with the blood of the many deceased after the battle. This enabled Ashoka to realise the magnitude of the horror associated with war.

He built several *Chaityas*, Stupas and pillars there. On top of the hill, a dazzling white peace pagoda of Lord Buddha has been built by the Japan Buddha Sangha and the Kalinga Buddha Sangha in 1970. We went there innumerable times, and each time, one could feel the peace and tranquillity in this hill. I always liked going there.

Puri was so near that we used to go on weekends. On Saturdays, Father would come back home early. We would go there and spend some time there on the beach and come back. We would make multiple visits to Puri. On one occasion, I was privileged to witness the *Rath*

Yatra from a vantage point. More of that later.

Puri is also known as Sri Jagannath Dhama after the 12th century Jagannath temple located in the city. It is one of the original Chardham pilgrimage sites for the Hindus. Puri is known by several names since ancient times and was locally known as "Sri Kshetra." The Lord Jagannath Temple is known as *"Badaduela."* Puri and Jagannath temple have been invaded 18 times by the Hindu and Muslim rulers from the 4th century AD till early 19th century with the objective of looting the treasures of the temple.

The Puri beach, or for that matter Puri, has an attraction which you cannot resist. You will find tourists throughout the year. I have been to Puri at least 15 times even after leaving Bhubaneswar - with parents, with family, with friends and relatives. Every time you touch Puri, you feel happy, and you feel the sea. You feel at peace with yourself.

My mother and grandmother wanted to see the Holy *Rath Yatra* which happens in the month of July every year.

Rath Yatra or chariot festival refers to the annual festival in Puri involving the public procession with a chariot of Lord Jagannath (avatar of Lord Vishnu), Balbhadra (his brother or Balarama) and his sister Subhadra. All these three chariots are *Raths* They are beautifully decorated, and resemble the structure of temples. Before the *Rath Yatra* starts, the King becomes the sweeper and sweeps the floor of the platform with a golden broom. The *Rath* then starts the journey towards the Gundicha temple via the Mausi ma temple (aunt's House).

This distance is 2 km from the main temple. The chariots are pulled by strong ropes. This festival attracts millions of Hindu pilgrims, and it is considered auspicious to pull the ropes of the Chariots. For this, lakhs of people risk their lives in pulling the ropes.

We were lucky to view this *Yatra* from a vantage point. We stood in the terrace of a building on the main road. It was a UBI back branch and the residence of the Branch Manager who had made all arrangements for us to see the *Yatra* clearly. From where we were located, one can see a sea of people in the road, and all of them were trying to pull the ropes. The chariots would be pulled at intervals. When the ropes were pulled, it was accompanied by the chanting of the Lord's name. It was a different feeling. The *Rath* would slowly make its way to the *Gundicha* temple. It would stay there for a week and make its way back to the main temple. This return journey was known as *Bahuda Yatra* or *Ulta Rath*.

There is another interesting story associated with the *Rath Yatra*. Lord Jagannath undertakes this journey to his maternal place with brother Balram and sister Subhadra. However, he does not take his wife, Ma Lakshmi for this journey. Ma Lakshmi has a separate temple within the precinct. She is very annoyed and does not allow Lord Jagannath to enter the temple once he returns from his maternal place after a week. However, after much convincing, she finally allows Lord Jagannath to enter the temple after one day. This ritual is still followed to date.

The pilgrimage to Puri is not complete without a visit to *Sakshi Gopal* which is about 20 Kms away from Puri. Hence, we also stopped at Sakshi Gopala. The temple looks like a miniature form of the Jagannath Temple.

There is a very interesting story behind Sakshi Gopala, and it does make for an interesting read.

It is said that that the deity of Gopala here had been originally installed by King Vajra, the grandson of Lord Krishna of Vrindavan long ago. Later, the deity walked all the way from Vrindavan to a place called Vidyanagar in South India to end a dispute between the Brahmans by being a witness. Thus, the deity has come to be known as *Sakshi* (witness) Gopala.

The story goes like this. Once, an old Brahmin decided to go on a pilgrimage along with a young Brahmin to Vrindavan. The youth helped the old Brahmin to have a *darshan* of Gopala. Pleased by the efforts of the youth, the old Brahmin promised to give his daughter's hand in marriage. However, after returning home, on pressure from his wife and son, he went back on his promise. The son of the old Brahmin said that he would agree to the marriage if the Lord would come and bear witness to the promise of his father.

The youth accepted the challenge and went to Vrindavan and prayed to Lord Gopala Krishna to come with him. The deity finally agreed on one condition that the youth should not look back while the deity followed him and the youth will know about his presence by the jingle of Lord's leg-bangles. Finally, when they reached the border of his village, the youth could not hear the jingle anymore since the Lord's feet were in the sand and the bangles did not give out the jingling sound. As soon as the youth turned back, the Deity stood still without moving further. The youth then immediately ran into the village and informed the people about Krishna's arrival as the witness. It is here on this spot a temple was built which came to be known as Sakshi Gopala. The King of Orissa then brought the deity from Vidyanagar and installed it in his fort in Cuttack. Sri Chaitanya Mahaprabhu visited the temple on his way to Puri. Thereafter, the deity was worshipped for some time in Jagannath temple. Later, the king of Orissa, Prataparuda installed the deity in the present location.

While we went to Puri on a number of occasions, we did not visit the Jagannath temple every time. It is one of the great *"Char Dham"* pilgrimage site found at India's four cardinal parts. Unlike the stone and metal idols found in most Hindu temples, the image of Jagannath is made of wood and is ceremoniously replaced every 12 or 19 years by an exact replica. The Temple was initially a Jain temple. Later on, a temple was constructed by the Kalinga king Indradyummna and rechristened it as Lord Jagannath. It was declared as the incarnation of Lord Vishnu. Later on, the present magnificent temple was built there by King Chadaganga of Eastern Ganga Dynasty in between late 11th century and early 12th century. The Temple has been invaded and plundered eighteen times. Many great saints such as Ramananda and Ramanuja have been associated with the temple.

Sri Chaitanya Mahaprabhu had spent his last 24 years in the Jagannath temple singing the praise of Lord Krishna, and slowly, he had a huge band of devotees. There are certain mysteries associated with the disappearance of Sri Chaitanya. The followers of Chaitanya believe that he merged with the Jagannath Deity or he jumped into the sea out of sorrow.

According to some literary sources, the left foot of Sri Chaitanya was injured while dancing, and it became the primary cause of death. In the last few years, a few scholars have done research on this topic. According to them, Sri Chaitanya was murdered in the temple, and his body was hidden within the Tota Gopnath temple precinct.

The ministers of the King of Orissa were angry with Mahaprabhu since the King as getting greatly influenced by Sri Chaitanya and started neglecting the affairs of the state. Also, the Oriya Brahmins were envious of him because of his popularity amongst Oriya devotees. Furthermore, there was a conflict between Oriya and Gaudiya (Bengali) devotees regarding whom would be considered as Mahaprabhu- the Deity of Lord Jagannath or Sri Chaitanya himself. Considering all these aspects, the researcher, Dr. Biman Bishnu Majumdar, has concluded that the disappearance of Mahaprabhu was not a natural incident.

The temple has many mysteries which does not have any scientific explanations. In fact, we have on many occasions been to the temple but failed to notice them. However, if one looks and studies the temple carefully, it would be stark in its reality.

The flag on top of the temple always floats in the opposite direction of the wind.

1800 years of ritual - Everyday a priest climbs the dome of the temple which is as tall as a 45 storeyed building and changes the flag. This has been continuing for the last 1800 years. The ritual says that if the flag is not changed for any day, then the temple must be shut down for the next 18 years.

The Sudarshan Chakra at the top of the temple is 20 feet in height and weighs a ton. The interesting thing is that one can see the chakra from any corner of the city. The installation of the chakra has been done in such a way that you can feel the Chakra facing you irrespective of your position.

The engineering structure of the temple was so unique that the shadow of the main dome could not be observed at any time.

In any place on Earth, the wind blows from the sea to land and vice versa in the evening. But in Puri, the opposite occurs.

Nothing flies above the temple. At any temple in India, birds fly and sit atop the temple except the Jagannath temple.

Every day, 2000 to 20,000 devotees visit the temple,

but the quantity of *prasadam* cooked in the temple remains the same throughout the year. None of the days would it go insufficient or wasted.

The Prasadam is cooked in earthen pots on firewood. Exactly, 7 pots are put on top of one another, and the topmost pot gets cooked first followed by the bottom pot in order.

There are 4 doors of the Jagannath temple. Singhadwaram is the main door to the temple. When you first enter the step of the Singhadwaram, you cannot hear the sounds of waves, but when you turn and walk back in the same direction, you can hear the sound of the waves. No sound can be heard until you come out of the temple.

The *prasad* is called *mahaprasadm,* and we have taken the *prasad* on some occasions from the precincts of the temple. *Mahaprasad* is used by Oriyas on many religious and social occasions, and it is served to the guests.

If you are in Puri, how can you miss the sea? The entire day, we would laze around the sea, going in the sea. Except for father, none of us knew how to swim. He would go deep into the sea. We would go inside, but we never ventured too deep into the sea. My *Thakuma,* (grandmother) who used to stay with us, would also come with us and take a dip in the sea. There were Nuliyas who would also take you deep into the sea. The sea is very rough at the side where the waves break and splash. If you are not careful, you can fall down and hurt yourself badly. In the middle of the sea, it is calm, and you can really enjoy the sea. Of course, the food at Puri was and still is awesome with various kinds of sea fish like crabs, pomfrets and Hilsa as well.

However, when we were at Bhubaneswar, it was very rare that we stayed overnight since it was only a 30 to 45-minute road journey. It was only much later when we were in Kolkata that we would plan a 3 to 4-day trip to Puri.

A lot of times, we would go to Konark which is about 35 Kms from Puri. Like Puri, we visited Konark on innumerable occasions with family, relatives and friends. It is also an architectural marvel. It is believed that the sea was right there where the temple is. The temple was built by King Narasimhadeva I of the great Ganga dynasty in the 13th century from 1243 to 1255 with the help of 1200 artisans. These artisans were not allowed to go home, and they were asked strictly to abstain from meat, wine and women during the course of this construction.

The stones used for constructing the temple are not found in this area, and it is evident that this was brought from far off areas. It is very difficult to imagine the logistics to make this huge temple. However, the sea has now receded. Dedicated to Lord Surya, what remains of the temple complex has the appearance of 100-foot-high Chariot with immense wheels and horses, all carved out of stone. Much of it is in ruins. This has been attributed to natural reasons like the winds of the sea which are salty and have eroded the stones, to the various deliberate destructions of the temple by Muslim armies between the 15th and the 17th centuries. This temple was called Black Pagoda because its great tower appeared black. Similarly, the Jagannath temple is called the White Pagoda.

The name, Konark, is derived from the combination of Sanskrit words Kona (corner or angle) and *Arka* (Sun). The Konark temple was built from stone in the form of a giant ornamental chariot. The architecture is also symbolic with the chariot's twelve pairs of wheels corresponding to the 12 months of the Hindu calendar. Other major works of art include sculptures of Hindu deities, *apsaras* and images from daily life and culture of the people. The erotic structures found in the temple's *shikaras* illustrate all the mudra forms described in the Kamasutra.

We used to get embarrassed in our childhood, when we were with our parents, to be in front of these sculptures. However, we would see a lot of young couples look at them with a lot of interest. The guides would also explain the sculptures to them in great detail.

The temple was so built that the first ray of the Sun would fall on the gigantic Sun idol kept inside the main temple complex.

One of the most fascinating things about this temple is that the Sun idol was suspended in the air and there were magnets used in the construction. So, when you enter the main temple, you'd see the tall idol in mid-air. For many years, it was a mystery. However what people did not realise that it was the magnetic field from all sides that made it happen. It is believed that the magnetic field affected the compass navigation for sailors when they were invading India. They ordered the magnets to be removed. So, the Idol could no longer be suspended in air.

Today, tourists are not allowed in the main chamber as it has been sealed. What remains today are a few structures, an open-air dance hall, and a dining hall. The Konark Dance festival is held here annually.

There are attempts being made to reconstruct and preserve this architectural marvel. However, one can clearly see the difference between the engravings which are being made on the wheels or on the temple body with the original engravings and sculptures. It is not much of a match. Large trees have been planted across the sea so that the salty wind cannot corrode the stones any further.

There is another story about Konark.

As we know, it took 1200 sculptors 12 years to make the temple. But, the temple was not getting finished. The King had given a deadline, and if the deadline was missed, all of them would be killed. A young boy named Dharma, son of the main sculptor came to meet his father whom he had not seen since his birth. However, when he came to the site, he came to know about the issue. They were not able to place the final stone atop the shrine. Dharma climbed atop. He noticed an architectural defect. After fixing the defect, he had had the stone fixed.

However, other sculptors were still not happy. They knew that once the King became aware of this, he would not be kind to them. If the small boy could rectify this, why were they not able to do so. Once the boy heard about this, he climbed to the top and jumped to commit suicide so that the King would never come to know about this incident.

There was another architectural marvel which was very near to our house from Sahidnagar namely, Udaigiri and Khandagiri Caves.

These are finely and ornately carved caves built during the 2nd century BC during the reign of King Kharvela. These caves were supposedly built for the abode of Jain ascetics

Now if we are talking about the city, let us talk about the food. Oriyas love to have something called *Pakhala Bhaat* which is simply water rice. The Oriyas love to have this in summers with *Bhaji* or *Subji* and chillies. This is very similar to what Bengalis have in the form of *Panta Bhat*.

In sweets, one of the most famous was *Chena poda* which is a cheese desert and immensely favourite. While I never used to like sweets, everyone else in our family would love to have it. I was more interested in the *aloo bada* and *pakoras* which we used to get in Sahidnagar. Who can forget Gojas which you would get in Puri and Bhubaneswar? Now, it is a ritual for any family to go to Puri and get Gojas.

Another memory which is still fresh in my mind even after 39 to 40 years is our family trip from Bhubaneswar to Kashmir. I am very happy and sad today since it happened to be my only visit to the "Paradise" on earth. I have not been able to take my wife and daughter to this place which is a dream destination.

Even today, when I think about that trip, I am amazed at the simplicity and the low cost which we incurred while having a high on enjoyment and memories. We undertook this trip with our *Pishi* (paternal aunt) and our cousins – Shankar and Mita. We first went from Bhubaneswar to Delhi in Nilachal Express. We went to Muradnagar where our Pisha and Pishi used to stay. Pisha (Uncle) decided to stay back. So, our gang of 9 went from Muradnagar to Delhi, and again from Delhi to Jammu. This time, however, we travelled in 3tier.

Travelling by train was always a great experience. We brothers would always fight for the window seat, and there would be a mad rush to occupy the window seats. Finally, each one of us would take turns to sit at the window seats. We would also buy some comics like Phantom, Indrajal, and we would finish reading them in a jiffy. The tiffin careers with food will always be there, and we would eagerly wait for the tiffin to be opened and the newspapers to be rolled out to keep our plates. Of course, the holdalls would have our blankets, bed sheets and pillows. In the night, the holdall will be opened, and the beds would be made. Travelling by rail was an amazing experience. Given a chance and time, I still like to travel by train. However, many of the things are missing today.

We finally reached Jammu in the evening. However, we found that there were no buses in the evening, and it was only available in the mornings. Jammu to Srinagar was a 10 to12 hour journey by road. We could have stayed in a hotel for the night, but we did not, and we decided to spend the night at the railway station only. The bus depot was near to the railway station. Hence, that would have been the reason. We also did not want to spend more money on a hotel since we were on a shoestring budget.

We bought the bus tickets for the morning. Then, we had dinner in the station which consisted of amazing *chola bhaturas*. We then slept in the railway station on the floor by getting the bed sheets and pillows from the holdalls! The best part was that nobody grumbled about it and we had three ladies in our group as well. Well, when I think of this, it looks totally unthinkable today. Our children, nor us would spend a night at the railway station.

We had a great time sleeping in the railway station.

The next morning, we started on our journey to Srinagar. The journey is beautiful, and the scenic beauty so lovely that 10 hours just passed by.

Finally, in the evening, we reached Srinagar - the paradise on earth. We then moved to a small Bengali Hotel which we had booked earlier. It was owned by a Bengali, and we got ourselves one large room!

All nine of us stayed in one room. I still cannot imagine as to how nine of us fitted into one room with only one washroom!

Our journey in Kashmir had begun. I would not remember all the details. However, we went around the Dal lake. I am not sure whether we had a *shikara* ride. But, we went to the Shankaracharya temple.

We also saw the famous Shalimar garden and Nishat Bag which were built by Jehangir and Noor Jahan. Emperor Jahangir and Noor Jahan were so enamoured by Kashmir that they travelled 13 times to Srinagar during the summers. The garden is exquisitely beautiful with flowers and fountains.

Amir Khusro, the Persian poet, once said about Kashmir, "If there is any paradise on earth, it is here, it is here, it is here."

After Srinagar, we would now undertake trips to Gulmarg, Khilenmarg and Sonmarg. We never stayed at these places, and we would undertake a day-long journey. We would be back in the evening in Srinagar.

We first started for Sonmarg (Meadow of gold) in a bus early morning. Sonmarg is located about 87 km from Srinagar. We passed through Nailah Sindh, which is a famous tributary of river Jhelum. It is upwards of 60 miles at an altitude of 2800 meters above sea level, which opens grassy meadow land and village dotted slopes.

Sonmarg has no permanent settlement and becomes inaccessible during winters due to heavy snowfall and avalanches.

Sonmarg has historical significance and was the gateway on ancient Silk Road along with Gilgit connecting Kashmir with Tibet. It still has a base camp for Ladakh and is strategically important for Indian army for the defence of Ladakh. We had obviously gone in the month of May. Hence, it was cold but pleasant. However, the entire valley was snow-clad, and if I remember, we rented special shoes for the snow. We hired ponies to take us to a higher place (which probably was the Thajiwas glacier). On top, we rented a sledge cart and had a great time on the snow.

Kashmiris, back then, were honest and innocent people. However, I have heard that they fleece the tourists in these places and charge exorbitant rates for everything.

After spending the day, we returned in the evening to Srinagar.

We also undertook visits to Gulmarg and Khilenmarg which are beautiful valleys adorned with flowers in the summers. However, we could not see snow here. Khilenmarg is 6 km away from Gulmarg. Gulmarg also has an 18 – hole golf course which is visited by many tourists to escape the heat and play a game of Golf.

We were totally mesmerised by the beauty of its valleys, flower-filled meadows and snow. This was the first time that we saw snow-capped valleys and hills, albeit in some places and at some altitudes.

The visit to Kashmir will always be etched in my memory not only by its pristine beauty but also by the fact that nine of us had made the trip which was not luxurious but immensely enjoyable.

However, the food at the guest house took its toll. Though they used to give Bengali food, the quality of the oil and other ingredients were suspect. Everyone had some kind of issues, and it was triggered while we were on our way back to Jammu on a bus.

Mejda had severe stomach upset and could barely sit. The bus had to be stopped, and he ran looking for a place to relieve himself near a spring. There are multiple springs on the way from Srinagar to Jammu. After many such encounters and having medicines, we finally reached Jammu station in the evening. Our train to Delhi was slated to leave in the night.

While Mejda had stopped going to the loo, he was still not ok. However, we were surprised that in dinner, he still wanted to have the delicious *Chana Bhatura*. Just imagine!

However, his demand was rightfully rejected by Pisima (aunt), and he was given only chura with water and lemon. He had to have that grudgingly.

This brought to an end one of my own amazing trips, and we returned to Bhubaneswar.

It was in Bhubaneswar that I learnt to ride a bicycle, and very quickly, I was riding one. We had a couple of bicycles, and we used to ride it throughout the city to school, and too far off places as well. This was a very good means of transportation since there were very few buses, and we did not have a bike. Father had a bank car which he used for his office work and his tours. We used the car on our trips to Puri and other places.

Ma also did a diploma course in food processing like making squash, Jam, jelly and marmalade. She did a 6-month course, and very soon, she became an expert. She made raw mango squash and made bottles of them along with Jam and jelly. The squash, jam and jelly were really good, and she used to distribute to others as well since she made in large quantities. Her quality and taste were very good. However, she never commercialized it. I still wonder, that if it was today, it could have been done with proper packaging and marketing.

While we were in the city of temples, there was a big noise over the crash of Skylab. For those who are unaware of what Skylab was, it was an orbiting workshop for scientific research which was designed for 9 years. However, NASA had not designed its smooth return, and in 1979, Skylab was decaying rapidly. It had become a 77-metric tonne of a loose cannon which was hurtling towards the earth.

There was tension all round that the Skylab could hit India as well including Bhubaneswar and Orissa.

Finally, NASA worked on the same and major part of the Skylab went into the Indian Ocean; some portions fell on Western Australia. Fortunately, no one was hurt. We also had a sigh of relief. Those days, there was no internet, and there was no bombardment of news and information. Hence, our information about the incident was limited and restricted. This led to increased tension.

Two sporting incidents are also etched in my memory from our Bhubaneswar stint. One was the India - England test match. It was the 4th test match at the Oval with India having lost the first test, and the other 2 being draws. This series was taking place after the 2nd World Cup where India failed miserably again. They were defeated by Sri Lanka!

On the 4th day, India needed 438 runs in the 4th innings and India made a solid start with Gavaskar and Chetan Chauhan being unbeaten at 76 for no loss.

We were glued to our radio - our old and reliable

Murphy radio. Our father was a great cricket enthusiast as well, and it was probably a Sunday. By afternoon, India were 213 for no loss and the chance was real. Finally, Chetan Chauhan was dismissed, and Dilip Vengsarkar came to join Gavaskar, and they took the score to 328 for 1 before the mandatory 20 overs needing just 110 runs. Going by today's standard, it was easy stuff. However, it is here that drama unfolded. The combination of Botham and bad umpiring by the British umpires robbed India of a sure shot victory and took them to a near defeat. Finally, India ended 9 runs short, and the test match ended in a thrilling draw. Sunil Gavaskar made a majestic double hundred of 221 runs; one of the finest innings in a run chase in a test match.

All of us brothers and Father were totally devastated that India could not beat the English which was a very rare phenomenon those days.

Another sports event was the gold at the Men's hockey tournament in the Moscow Olympics. However, this win was taken with a pinch of salt since this Olympics was boycotted by America and it did not have the powerhouses of hockey like Germany, Holland, Australia, New Zealand and Pakistan. Though a gold was expected from India, it did not enjoy smooth sailing. India also had a very young team led by Bhaskaran. The team had very talented young individuals like Md Shahid and Zafar Iqbal. India finally defeated Spain 4–3 to win the Gold and Md Shahid turned out to be a star. He was someone in the mould of Dhyan Chand with his super stick work.

As a Hockey fan, we were again glued to our radio and heard the game live which was made livelier by Jasdev Singh, the ace Hindi commentator whom I have described earlier in this book.

There was another sporting incident where India took centre stage. Prakash Padukone defeated Lim Swi King of Indonesia in the All England Badminton championship. This was a game dominated by the Indonesians, Chinese and the Malaysians and also the Danes to an extent. Prakash Padukone was an artist, and he was the player who made badminton popular in the country which would see India becoming a major force after 35 years

As I have mentioned earlier, Father had a touring job and Mother used to accompany him in many of his visits. In many such trips, she would insist that I should accompany her as well if the schedule was for more than 1 day. She was very protective of me always.

I remember one such trip which was to Sambalpur and the Hirakud dam. We were put up in the Orissa Guest House which was atop the Hirakud Dam. The dam is built across the Mahanadi river about a few km from Sambalpur. While Father was in a meeting, we stayed in the guest house suite. It was a fantastic suite with all amenities. But, Mother had this strange habit of washing clothes even in the hotel, even if the stay was for a day!

In the evening, we ordered for chicken butter masala which was yum. However, fearing that it might not be good and I would fall sick, she did not allow me to have

132

much of it, and she discarded the entire thing in the dustbin!

She was not aware of this preparation of chicken butter masala, and she did not like the idea of so much cream in the dish!

Dada (brother) would come from the hostel. He was a handsome young man now. Mejda also had a smart look about him. He had long hair and looked rough and tough. Sejda was dark, strong and lanky. We had good bonding amongst ourselves, and we were there for each other.

When all 4 brothers were in the house, we needed no one, and the house was always alive.

When I reflect on those days which are gone, and when I look at the present situation, I feel sad. Today, we are in 4 different cities, and on very rare occasions, we come together. It was only during my niece's wedding which is almost 4 ½ years back that we 4 brothers had come together with our families. While technology has brought us closer, the feeling has gone out of brotherhood. Maybe, I am wrong, but I would be happy to be proven wrong.

One fine day in July 1980, we heard that Uttam Kumar, the famous and legendary Bengali actor, had passed away due to a heart attack. My mother was a big Uttam Kumar fan, and she was deeply saddened by the sudden demise of the "*Mahanayak*."

We four brothers were not so much a fan of him, or for that matter, Bengali cinema, as we were not exposed to

Bengali cinema to that extent. It was only after we came to Kolkata and got exposed to Bengali cinema, did we realise what a great actor Uttam Kumar was. I have watched many of his movies, and I also became a big fan of this very great actor. His films like "*Nayak*" by Satyajit Ray are true flawless exhibitions of great acting.

He was superb in this movie, and very few in the Indian film industry would be able to replicate the high standard of acting which he displayed in this movie. Among his many classics, which I saw later, were films like *Antony firangi, Saptapadi, Sanyasi Raja, Chiriayaghar,* etc. He could not make a mark in Hindi Cinema due to his poor diction in the Hindi language. In fact, I was deeply pained by his role in "Desh Premee" where the hero was Amitabh Bachchan. This was a very poor role given to a great man and with poor execution. Till date, I have not understood as to why he did this movie.

Our journey of the iconic "Feluda" movie series by Satyajit Ray started in Bhubaneswar when we saw "Joy Baba Felunath." Over the years, we would just love to see movies like "Sonar Kella." It was directed by Satyajit Ray and Soumitra Chatterjee essaying the role of Feluda. It is said that Satyajit Ray wrote the character of Feluda keeping in mind Soumitra Chatterjee. Later on, his son, Sandip Ray would carry on the tradition of Feluda and make multiple Feluda movies with Sabyasachi Chatterjee as Feluda. It was only after watching Feluda that I started reading all Feluda novels penned by the great Satyajit Ray.

As is the case previously, a lot of relatives came to visit

us in Bhubaneswar since this is a very attractive tourist spot. Mama, Mami and my cousins, Pisha, Pisima and cousins and many others visited us in Bhubaneswar not only to see the city but also to visit Puri and other places of attraction.

Our time was again up. Father had asked the management that he wanted to settle down in Calcutta finally, and build a house there post-retirement. While in Durgapur, he had purchased a 4 cottah plot in Salt Lake (Bidhan Nagar) in Kolkata under lottery system for just Rs. 8000 per Cottah. It was a very wise decision since, in today's market, each Cottah of the plot in Salt Lake has a valuation of 1 Cr plus.

The management agreed to his request, and he was transferred to Calcutta as a Regional Manager for South Kolkata region. While I was never critical of anything my father did, this movement again affected me the most. Dada was in his last year in engineering in BIT Mesra, and in a year's time, he would graduate. Mejda had passed his class XII from Central school, and he got admitted to BJB college with Maths Hon's and stayed back in the hostel there. He would later graduate from there. Sejda had no issues since he would get admitted to Central school at Fort William in Kolkata. It was me again who was going to get impacted since it was again in the middle of the session, and I would not get admitted to any school in Kolkata. Hence, I would again lose out another year. I wanted to be kept back in Bhubaneswar, but my parents did not agree.

Even if I never felt bitter about it, I was disappointed since I lost out 2 years due to frequent transfers of my father.

One of my best memories of childhood apart from my stay in Agra and Patna was that of Bhubaneswar. Not only did I enjoy my stay in the city, but I also loved my school after the initial hiccup was over. I made some very good friends there. I was a good sportsman, and I was playing well in cricket.

Many years later, when I went to Bhubaneswar on an official trip to finalise a premise for a branch for my bank, I went to my old school. The summer holidays were on. I roamed around the school, and it was a feeling of nostalgia which engulfed me.

The entire process started. We started packing. Mejda accompanied me to my school and got the TC. I bid goodbye to all my friends and teachers. I was especially close to Chinmay. We had dinner at their house as well before leaving the city. We promised to write to each other. We continued to write to each other for a long time. Then, suddenly, one day, the letters stopped from both ends, and we lost touch. It was recently that we gained connection thanks to Facebook. He currently stays in the US, and he passed out from IIT Kharagpur.

We also bid goodbye to the family of Shome with whom we had such good relations that they had become family. However, in the later period, the relations were slightly strained.

Father, as usual, had gone earlier. While there, he rented a place in Salt Lake (CA Block). He wanted to stay in Salt Lake since that is where our plot of land was, and it would be easier to build the house from there.

Once the truck left our house with all stuff, we also packed our bags, and it was time to bid goodbye to the wonderful city of temples and move to a Metro city- the city of Calcutta.

10. Kolkata

We came to Kolkata. Our house in Salt Lake was very small - maybe about 600 square feet only. This was the smallest house which we ever lived in. Maybe, this was reflective of our stay in Kolkata which was going to be totally different from the places where we lived right from schools, the standard of living, the city bustle and people.

Since the house was very small, Thakuma (grandmother) was not able to stay with us anymore, and she had to stay with my younger Pisima (paternal aunt) who was staying in Bali. This should no be confused with another city of Bali which is in Indonesia! This is a suburb in Kolkata near Belur.

This was the beginning of our ordeal in Calcutta or Kolkata. Father had joined his office. Mejda was in Bhubaneswar completing his science graduation. Sejda had got admitted to the Central school. It was me only who was doing nothing since I had no option but to wait for the next academic session. I used to spend time reading books and listening to the radio. Those days, there were many dubbed Bengali programmes like Sherlock Holmes and Arabian nights. There were many interesting programmes, and radio used to be our only source of entertainment. We also used to play cricket in the locality with boys of the same locality. But, we were missing on the quality and competitive sports which we were exposed to earlier.

Finally, the next academic session arrived. Unfortunately, around this time, my Grandmother fell sick as well.

Father would travel all the way to Bally from office, and would then, come back. He was getting frustrated since Thakuma was not recovering and she was not being given the best of the medical attention that she needed. On top of that, he was not able to bring her to his house. Finally, one day, Thakuma expired. That was probably the first time that I saw my father crying. In fact, the earlier night, he claimed that Thakuma had come to his bedroom, and was calling him. He knew that she was no longer there. We all went to Bally. Thakuma was cremated.

However, during this time, we had to go to different schools as well. I remember having gone to St Thomas Howrah. I sat for an entrance exam. I do not remember clearly. It seems that I was not selected. We then approached St Lawrence School. However, everything was over, and the entrance exam was also over. My father requested the principal to take cognizance of the fact that Thakuma had expired, and hence, we were not able to make it. However, the Principal did not relent.

Finally, we went to St Mary's school in Dum Dum which was a Missionary school. My father went to the meet the Principal, Brother Malcauy. He was a nice gentleman who agreed to take my test. I passed the test, and I was admitted to class VIII A. I had to repeat class VIII again in a different city. But, at least, I had a school to go now. It was a good school with 2 very large playgrounds, a very neat and clean school and a very good library.

I used to go to school in a local train from Ultadanga station. It was just one station to Dum Dum where my school was located. I acquired a monthly ticket so that I need not get into the hassle of buying a ticket every day.

Our class teacher in class VIII A was Richard Payne. He was a good teacher and he strict as well. Those days, discipline was very strong, and we used to get canned very frequently. Today, parents create so much of hue and cry over punishments. I used to come with Parthasarathi Senshama. However, he used to get late very often, and he would either get caned or had to stand outside the class. There was another fellow student, Govinda Pal who was a short fellow with a very sweet face. He used to wear another pant below his school pant so that, when he got caned, it would not hurt. Many of the boys wore half pants. However, I started to wear full pants.

Very soon I realised that I was not able to see the blackboard, and I had to start wearing spectacles.

I was good in studies. Hence, the class teacher started liking me. I also made a lot of friends in the class. Apart from Partha and Govinda, I made friends with Harish Pillai, Prasunjit Mukherjee, Abir Ghosh, Mrinmoy Mullick, Angshu Bhowmik, Siddhartha Kar Gupta and others whom I became close over a period of three years.

I also started playing cricket. Very soon, I was part of the team and started playing regularly. However, I stopped playing football and concentrated on table tennis.

Two things became very clear to me. I was not the same student anymore, and I was not the same cricketer as well. Somehow, I did not have the same rhythm as I had once had while bowling in Bhubaneswar, and my pace had dropped significantly. My batting was also not the same. Maybe, lack of practice had led to this. In Bhubaneswar, I was playing cricket every day, and I used to be in good rhythm. Though I continued playing cricket actively till class XII, it was no longer the same. Also, my eyesight was not as good as it used to be.

I was also not the same student. While I was still a good student, I suddenly slipped from 1st, 2nd position to being 5th in the section. I released that Maths was a problem, and so was Physics and Chemistry. I was suddenly exposed to ICSE board which was far tougher than the CBSE board. I used to like English - both literature and history.

I got promoted to class IX, and my woes with Maths and science continued. I still remember that we had a thick Physics book of Abbot which I was not able to crack, and Trigonometry and Arithmetic were getting tougher and tougher. To compound my woes, our class IX Maths teacher was Brother Kyle, an Irish gentleman for whom I was scared out of my wits. This is the time when I started hating him and started hating Maths. When I look back, I was not bad in Maths, but it was probably lack of guidance and my fear of the Maths teacher which led to that situation. On one hand, in class, Pillai would solve a maths problem in a jiffy, whereas I, sitting with him on the same bench, would struggle badly. Brother Kyle would come to our bench and have a look at both of us. It was enough for me to give in to the tension, and I would falter further.

This fear was playing havoc with me. I started bunking school on the pretext of stomach ache, especially on days when there was Maths or when I had not been able to complete my homework.

On one occasion, I came out of home but did not go to school. I went to a park a little far away from our home, and I spent the entire day in the park just sitting!

On another occasion, I went to school but did not enter the school. Instead, I took a train and bus to go to Sealdah and saw a movie instead. After watching the movie, I went home.

This went on for some time before my parents took notice, and I told them about my fear. I do not remember as to what happened post that. Somehow, I made it to class X.

Thankfully, Brother Kyle was no longer teaching us Maths, and Brother Fernandes was our class teacher. He was an excellent human being, and he used to teach us

English. He would also tell us stories very often, and these were mainly from Sydney Sheldon who was a master storyteller. By this time, I also used to write very well and was very good in English essays where I used all my imaginations effectively.

Once, our teacher had given us an essay on the Battle of Plassey. He gave it a twist asking us to write this as if we were present during that time, and it should be from our perspective. I remember my essay was very good and imaginative, and Brother Fernandes had praised me in the class. Apart from my style of writing, my handwriting was also very good. My father had beautiful handwriting, and even today at the age of 92, his handwriting is far better than any of our four brothers.

However, it was clear that science was not my cup of tea, and I would not opt for science after my board exams. The board exams happened, and I was disappointed with my marks. I got the first division with only 66% of marks, whereas, most of my friends had done exceedingly well.

I was not a student that deserved these kinds of marks. I still feel that if I had got proper guidance, I would have done much better than what I finally got.

I do not know as to what the feelings of my parents and brothers were. As a ritual though, I got my first HMT watch from my father

It was time again to move out to another school or college.

The SMO 84 batch (St Mary's Orphanage) was a super

batch with some brilliant students who have done a lot in their lives.

Partha Sen Sharma went to IIT and now is a Professor in IIT Lucknow. He has many patents after him.

Harish Pillai is IITian and is a Professor in IIT Mumbai.

Govinda is a director in TCS in London. Angshu, Mrinmoy are doctors settled in Kuwait and London. The list is endless.

By this time, Dada had graduated, and he got his first job in Bharat Electronics Ltd. He worked there for long, and very soon, he moved on to Escorts Ltd which was a company dealing in manufacture of tractors.

While we were in our first house at Salt Lake CA Block, we had our neighbours - the Sen Family - and we became very close to them. They had a son and a daughter. The son was a very good student in Don Bosco, and the girl was younger to me. On most Saturdays and Sundays, we used to go to their house. They had a black and white TV, and we used to watch a Bengali movie on Saturdays and Hindi movies on Sundays.

We did not have a TV in our house, and we could not go to their house on every occasion. With the World Cup football and Cricket test matches, we needed to find some other house as well.

Hence, we used to go another of our father's colleague's house who used to stay in a block close to us. We watched the entire World Cup football 1982 from their house. It was the first time that we saw World Cup football live. We saw the great Brazilian team, which to my mind was the greatest football team ever to have played with Zico, Socrates, Falcao and Edar. When they were playing, it was just like poetry in motion with such fluid and fast movements. I had never seen anything like this. This tournament also saw the emergence of Diego Maradona who was going to become the new Superstar of World Football. However, in this tournament, rival players did not allow him to play his normal game. He was fouled umpteen number of times and was brought down regularly and ruthlessly. This finally resulted in Diego fouling in frustration and being sent off the field. This also led to the ouster of Argentina who were the defending champions. The World Cup final was won by Italy who defeated Germany by 3–1 and Paoli Rossi, the Italian striker, was the hero.

However, the 1986 World Cup football belonged to one and only Diego Maradona. His speed and his footwork left the opposition in a daze, and Argentina defeated West Germany in the final 3 – 2. I would specifically remember the goal of Diego Maradona against Belgium where he took the ball from his own half and dribbled past 6 to 7 Belgians including the goalkeeper, and tapped the ball inside the goal. Many consider this as to the goal of the century. The 2nd goal was the apparent "hand of God" goal by Maradona against England. However, he also scored a superb 2nd goal against England.

This time, we watched the World Cup in colour and

from our own house since we had our own TV now. Father had purchased a colour EC TV just prior to the Delhi Asiad in 1982. Prior to that, people used to have Band W TV, and in order to get a flavour of the colour, many used to put a colour film on top of the screen!

By this time, we had again shifted our house another one in Salt Lake, But the house was in a different block. It was flat in a Cooperative of the bank. This was the first time we were staying in a flat in our lifetime. It was a bigger house than the earlier one.

In 1983, we had the good fortune to see the ICC World Cup cricket for the first time on TV. However, the Indian government decided to telecast only once India reached the semi-finals. Maybe, nobody gave India any chance considering the poor record which we had in 1975 and 1979 World Cups. However, the Indian team, under Kapil Dev, started on a strong note and upset the West Indies. We were following all matches though radio commentary. The classic match was between India and newcomers Zimbabwe. India was reduced to 17/5, and everything seemed lost. However, Kapil Dev played a dream innings of 175 and bailed India out. It was a hurricane innings. Fortunately, we could hear the live commentary of the match. Unfortunately, there was no TV recording in the ground where it was being played, and that innings has been lost forever. India marched into the finals of the Prudential Cup, and they were to clash with the two-time Champions, the West Indies. In the semi-final India easily defeated England, and this match was telecast live in India. We had had the good fortune to see the match.

All of us gathered in the room for the final match against West Indies at Lords and India batted first. India had no answer to the pace battery of the Windies, and they were bowled out for 183 with Srikanth being the highest scorer with 38. Those days, the One-day match was a 60 over the affair and getting 183 in 60 overs was a cakewalk. Vivian Richards wanted to end the game in 30 overs. However, Kapil Dev took a stunning catch running backwards to dismiss Richards and the slide begun. Indian bowlers bowled with guile including Amarnath who was swinging the ball prodigiously. The West Indies were bowled out for 140 odd runs, and Kapil's Devils had done the unthinkable.

There were huge celebrations at our house. I remember, it was around 10.30 pm or 11 pm in the night and, we could hear the sound of firecrackers in the street. It was midnight when Kapil Dev finally lifted the Cup, and the whole of India, including us, were delirious with joy. Cricket in India would never be the same again, and India would become a very strong team in the coming years. Everything associated with Cricket would change.

Our TV watching was not restricted to sports only. We used to watch all kind of sports from Cricket to football to hockey to Tennis including the Wimbledon. However, on the entertainment side, there was not much. Apart from the Bengali movie on Saturday and Hindi movie on Sunday, we used to wait for *Chitrahar* on Wednesday. It was a film song programme for 30 minutes. In those days, watching Hindi movie song standalone was a novel affair, and it was exciting. We used to wait eagerly for it.

However, load shedding (breakdown of power) would be the dampener on many occasions. The power would probably come only after the programme was over. Those days, power situation was very bad in Kolkata, and at times, the load shedding would continue for hours. Every house had a lantern, and we used to study using the lantern during these times of power break. Only the rich people had a generator, and even the generator cannot run for 6 to 8 hours. If any VIP died had during this period, there would be national mourning for 7 days when no entertainment programme would be aired.

That is the time we used to switch on to Bangladesh TV. There used to be a separate antenna for that, and somehow, it used to pick up signals from the Bangladesh Channel.

They used to show very good English serials. Some of the best serials I would have seen on this channel include Different Strokes, Dallas, Knight Rider and many more. Many of which I do not remember as of now.

At times, we would not get the signal, and we had to resort to various means to get the signal back involving going to the terrace and moving the antennae ever so slightly and manipulating the movement so that we could get the signal.

This was the time for Mega serials like Ramayana and Mahabharat. I specifically remember that Mahabharat used to be telecast on Sunday morning from 11 am for 1 hour. Everyone used to be glued to it. Everything stopped during this time, and the roads and streets used to be empty. We would also see street boys peeking from our windows to watch the telecast. No serial had ever seen such kind of viewing and attachment like Mahabharat. During the course of these years, Doordarshan came with many mega serials which were good in content and quality, and I can safely say that TV serials now are no match to those serials.

Some of these serials which are still etched in our memories, and given a chance, I would love to watch them again. I would like to name a few like Malgudi days, Hum Log, Buniyad, Circus, Fauji, Junoon, Dekh bhai dekh, Wagle Ki Duniya, Moongerilal ke hasin Sapney, Vikram aur betal, Chandrakanta, Tipu Sultan and many more.

The script was great, and the acting was top class. Many of the Hindi film personalities used to act in these serials, and many of the great actors in Bollywood started their journey from these serials. The biggest example is the "Badshah" of Bollywood, Shahrukh Khan who started his career with TV serials- Fauji and Circus.

The year I passed my class X, 1984, there was another incident which would rock the World. Mrs. Indira Gandhi, the Prime Minister of India, was shot by her own security guards in her official residence. This was in retribution the Operation Blue Star wherein the Indian army had stormed the Golden Temple in Amritsar and flushed out and killed the Khalistan militants including Jarnail Singh Bhindranwale. The religious sentiments of the Sikhs were hurt, and Mrs. Gandhi's assassination was a result of that. We were all shocked. I do not remember if it was a holiday or whether a holiday was declared. But, the days which followed the assassination and funeral of Mrs. Gandhi was a dark chapter in Indian history wherein a particular community was signalled out for mass killings, and it happened mostly in Delhi and in a sporadic manner across the country.

It was from this 2nd house in BB Block that I passed my class X. Then, I started looking for a college to do my plus 2. By this time, I had decided that I would pursue arts and not science. Those days we ourselves went to the colleges, stood in line for hours, took the applications, and then, completed and submitted the applications. I had applied for Arts in all the major colleges in Kolkata including St Xavier's, Scottish Church College and Maulana Azad. I got through in all of them. However, I decided to get admitted to St Xavier's College. Those days the best of the best students would go for Engineering and Medical, and the mediocre students would opt for Commerce. Finally, those who had no other option would go for Arts. Hence, it was Arts for me.

I started going to college and started enjoying it. It was a college of great repute and high educational standards. A few of my school friends also got enrolled in the science stream.

Class XI and XII were part of the college, but it was only in name. The college administration was very strict, and the classes were held regularly unlike many other colleges where classes were hardly held, and students whiled away their time. In our college, we needed to have a minimum 75% of attendance, and it was strictly adhered to. However, it did not stop us from sneaking out of the college and going for movies. We would usually bunk the 11.40 am class and go for the Noon show in either Metro, Globe, Tiger, New Empire or Lighthouse.

These are the halls where English movies would be screened, and this is the time I was exposed to Hollywood movies. I saw many great and good English movies. I remember we used to usually get Rs 2.40 or Rs 4 ticket in these halls! Now, with the advent of multiplexes, all these iconic movie halls have gone into oblivion, and they have been converted to shopping malls, etc. How did I manage to see all these movies?

I used to get about Rs. 3 to 4 every day for transport and lunch. Would save out of that and go for movies.

Today, a movie on the weekend would cost about Rs. 250.

We also learned to give a proxy to our friends who bunked. What is a proxy? Many of you may not know. It is basically giving attendance on behalf of your friend. When the Professor used to call out the Roll number, you would respond to the roll number of your friend is called. Many of the teachers would not look up while taking attendance. Hence, it was easy. However, it became very difficult with teachers who would look up while taking attendance.

Some of the vices also crept in me while studying in the college. I started smoking. Initially, it was just one puff or two from a friend's cigarette; then it became a habit. However, I never got addicted to it. I never became a compulsive smoker. Those days, there was the menace of drug abuse in almost all colleges, and ours was no different. Thankfully, my friends and I never went even remotely close to that, though we could see many students coming under its deadly influence.

I also took my first drink while I was in class XI. I started with beer which I first had in Tiger hall while going for a movie. Then, I used to have a beer once in a while. However, I was pretty smart and people back home never came to know that I used to smoke and drink. I always used to have masala or mint. I would make sure that by the time I reached home there would be no smell coming from my mouth.

My movie escapades were not only with my friends. I used to go for a lot of movies with my Sejda. We would either go to Esplanade to watch English movies, and College Street and Shyambazar for Hindi movies. We were pretty regular in that.

Amitabh Bachchan was at his peak, and we would never miss his movies. If required, we would buy tickets in black paying a higher amount.

In one such instance, we went to see a Bachchan movie. We went to a hall in College street to watch it. However, the show, as usual, was "Houseful." But, we were not in a mood to come back. We bought the tickets in black and enjoyed the movie. However, we had spent the entire amount on the ticket, and we had no money to come back! That did not deter us. Once the movie was over, we made our way back walking from College Street to Salt Lake! It is about 5 to 6 km, and we had to walk for probably one and a half hour to reach home.

Those days, buses to Salt Lake were very few, and if you missed, then you had to wait for a long time for another bus. Those buses used to be overcrowded with people hanging outside the bus as well in most cases. In one of our journeys back home, we caught a bus from College street. It was overcrowded, and to make it worse, the streets and roads were flooded after thunderstorms and rains. Once I got up on the bus, I was feeling unwell and could not breathe. I told my Sejda(brother) that I was not able to stay on the bus anymore and I wanted to come out. Sejda told me to stay put since the roads were flooded, it was raining, and we would not get another one. However, I did not listen to him and alighted from the bus straight into the waters and rains. Poor Sejda had no option but to come out as well. Then, we had to wade through the water, and walk for hours before we reached home!

By this time, Sejda was in Scottish Church College doing graduation with major in History. Mejda had finished his graduation in Mathematics. He was wondering what to do when my Bora Mama who is a Chartered Accountant himself suggested that he took that as well as a profession. CA Exam those days were very tough, and people used to take years to pass. Sometimes they would take 7 to 8 years to pass as well. Now kids are smarter, and many of them pass it one shot and clear in 3 years flat.

Mejda started the journey. It was tough. While he cleared part 1 easily, he found it extremely difficult to pass part 2, and it took him many years to clear the hurdle which he finally did after 7 long years. Over the years, we would see his frustration growing. As a result, anger was coming out mainly on my mother, and later on my Boudi (sister in law). However, my poor mother got the brunt of it. Most of us used to keep quiet since we could understand that he was going through a very bad phase.

In the interim, Dada had left Escorts and got into Maruti Udyog Limited. Till today, he is working in that organisation. Even after his retirement, he is on extension. He loves his job, he loves his company, and he is very passionate about his job and company.

Once we were in Kolkata, we could interact and meet with most of our relatives who were in the city, and we did.

However, there were some people who became very close with us. One was Abhijit da and his family including his wife Piku Boudi and their son Raja. Abhijit da was the boss of my eldest brother (Dada) while he was in Escorts. They used to live in the same Cooperative flat where we used to live, a few blocks away. Abhijit da had not got his family. My mother had told him to have dinner with us every day. So, whenever he was in the city, he would come after work, and have dinner with us. Those days were different. These things used to happen. Now, I don't think anyone will invite someone on a daily basis to have dinner or lunch or even to come on a daily basis. He or she would feel embarrassed. We led a simple life with no complexities.

This created a bond with Abhijit da which became strong over a period of time. He and his family later became part of our family, and we would not hesitate to share anything with him. Piku Boudi was a beautiful and intelligent woman who shared the same passion for good Hollywood movies and books. Hence, on many occasions, we would go to their house watch many movies on CD and exchange storybooks. Later on, when Dada got married, Piku Boudi became very close to Boudi (sister in law). Even today, the bond is there. They have now settled in Canada where they have for many years. Piku Boudi makes it a point to meet Dada and Boudi whenever she is in Delhi, and Abhijit would call me from Canada whenever he gets time.

There were times when Abhijit da would have lent money to father, and he never refused. Whether it was for building our house, or for marriage purpose, he was always there. Father obviously would return each and every paise. Again, how many of us would actually do that today?

The 2nd family and person who grew very close to us was our paternal cousin sister Mitradi and her husband, Anadi Roy. He was our Jamai Babu (brother- in law). He became a regular visitor to our house and was involved in all matters of our house. He stood behind us in every crisis and every requirement. He is a noble soul. He was an engineer and used to work with Indian telephones. He was a man who had a lot of talent. He was very good at yoga, very fit and knew about cooking and knitting. But, as happens with these kinds of people, they think they know everything and everyone.

But, whenever he used to visit, it was always fun to listen to his stories. Time just used to fly away. He used to tell us that in his younger days, he was a *Mastan* in Howrah, and people were scared of him. However, on the contrary, on to occasions we got proof that he was not at all that kind of person and was afraid of a lot of things. Once, when we were travelling by bus in the night from Kolkata to Giridih for our Dada's marriage, he was unwilling to come. We literally had to force him to come. The second instance was when my two brothers got embroiled in a fight, and there was the involvement of police, Jamai Babu was scared! I will talk about this in greater details a little later.

Father and Mother were now planning to get Dada married even though he was only 26 years old. Dada was vehemently against it. As luck would have it, the bride walked into our house on her own with her mother!

It was Kalyan Jethu's youngest daughter Sujata and Jethima (aunty) who one suddenly came to our house. She had turned out to be a beautiful lady, very fair and with long hair. We were all very impressed with her. My Dada was out of station during that time. My mother was the most impressed, and she asked her directly whether she would marry her son!

She naturally blushed and asked her to talk to her

mother. The process started, and finally, the marriage was fixed for November. There was great excitement in the house since this was the first marriage. Dada was shown the picture of Boudi (sister in law). I am sure he would have liked her beauty, but on the face of it, he still maintained that it was not the right time to get married. However, we knew he would agree, and he eventually did.

All the relatives came to our house. It was different those days. People used to stay in the same house even if it meant that people had to sleep on the floor. All our relatives, Boro Pisha and Pishi and our cousins, Choto Pisha and Pishi and our cousins, our Mama and Mami and Jethima and Jethu (Uncles and Aunts). There was a lot of planning every day which used to happen even 3 months before the marriage. It was great fun. The planning before the marriage has more fun than the marriage itself. There is a Bengali proverb which says, *"Lakh kotha Jodi no holo tahole ki biye holo?"* Which means that if you do not have lakhs of discussion before the marriage, what kind of marriage is this?

Those days catering service had not come into vogue. So, we had to arrange for a Cook. The entire responsibility was given to our Choto Pisha (Uncle) who had expertise in this. However, we were proved wrong. He ordered 50 Kg of fish, and 50 Kg of chicken along with other dishes and we had about 200 to 250 guests. There was huge wastage. For days together, we would eat those fish and chicken and fry. We distributed the rest in out para giving it our neighbours and friends. So much for expertise.

As usual, there were certain skirmishes between the two families over some issues. It all added spice to the wedding. The best part was that the wedding was not in Kolkata. It was going to be held in Giridih where the Ghosh family lived. So, a bus was provided for us to go. Many did not go since they did not want to travel through the night from Kolkata to Giridhih. Finally, some 20 of us went by Bus. It was great fun. We stopped in the night at a Dhaba and had very good food. Finally, early morning, we reached the destination. Reaching there, we had a sumptuous breakfast of *Luchhi*, *Tarkari* (Bengali Puri and Subji)

In the evening, we all got dressed and went to their residence where the marriage was supposed to be solemnised. The marriage happened late in the night, and Dada stayed back as is the ritual. We returned to the guest house.

Next day, in the early afternoon, we started from Giridih and reached Kolkata in the evening. My mother was there to greet the new bride, and as per customs and rituals, many games were played. In the following days, we had rented a VCR and cassettes and started seeing many movies back to back.

It was great fun. It was now time for all relatives and friends to go. It was time for the new bride and bridegroom to settle down and start a family.

My Boudi soon settled down. She made a lot of effort in our household, and she was involved in housework and cooking. However, it was a tough job to keep her in-laws happy. My father and mother were difficult. However, my Boudi worked hard on these relationships and tried her best to keep everyone happy. I became very close with her, and so was Sejda. We were always beside her whenever she needed us, especially if there was a tiff between her and Mother. She was a good student as well and had done her Post graduation. However, she wanted to do her B.Ed. and become a school teacher. A few years later, she would complete that. I always saluted her for this effort, because she did this after taking care of the household. We were a big family with 8 of us. By that time my niece was born, and she was small.

I supported her in whatever little way I could. Since I was very good in history, I would teach her history lessons which she found very useful. She finally managed to complete her B.Ed. course successfully. However, her relationship with my Mejda was not good. **Mejda's** behaviour towards her was a little rude. His behaviour towards Mother was the same as well. This was largely due to his frustration for not being able to clear his Chartered Accounts exam.

When my niece, Sumi, was born, she was the first child being born into our family after a long time. She became the life of our family, and we all used to love her very much. We used to pamper her in whatever little ways we could. She also became very close to me and was very fond of me. She used to call me "Chotka," the name by which my Boudi also used to call me. I am still her "Chotka" after so many years.

She was a hyperactive child, naughty and adventurous. When she grew up a little, she would go for all the adventure rides in the NICCO park which was a theme park in Salt Lake. She grew up to be a fantastic athlete, and that too at a national school level. She has won many medals and accolades. Her adventure streak is still very much there with her. It was evident in her honeymoon when she went to New Zealand and participated in many adventure sports with her husband, Neel. She had enjoyed bungee jumping, and jumping from the plane. She is a bundle of energy and enthusiasm. It feels nice to see her settled with her in-laws beautifully balancing her work and home, and more importantly her in-laws.

There were 2 incidents which happened while we were staying in the BB Block flat. Both of them happened while I was in college.

One day, while I returned from college, I found the house to be sombre.

My Boudi then narrated as to what had happened. It was raining in the afternoon when my mother was coming home, and the gate was closed. When the guard, who was a Nepali, was asked to open the gate, he suddenly started abusing my mother in a very bad way. Hearing that, my Sejda rushed out. However, the Nepali was much stronger, and he hit my Sejda in the eye, and he fell to the ground. My Mejda was also in the house. He rushed out and started battling with him. After a while, both were separated by onlookers. My brothers were seething in anger. However, they were brought inside the house by my mother.

Sejda was badly hit in the eye. I could see that he was barely able to open his left eye. Mother had started giving him hot water compression.

In the evening, Sejda went out to meet his friend, Surajit, who was his only friend and his classmate in College. Surajit came from a Zamindar family who had their lands in Bihar and Bengal. He helped his mother to look after their *Zamindari*. He was a tough guy, but very soft spoken. He would often come to our house.

When Surajit heard as to what had happened, and the fact that Sejda was hit, his blood was boiling, and he could not hold himself back. He rushed to our block with around 10 to 12 friends who had rods and chains as well.

The Nepali guard saw a bunch of guys rushing towards him and attempted to flee. But, it was late. Surajit was a tough fellow, and he pounced on the Nepali and started beating him up. The Nepali fell on the ground, and others started beating him up as well. In the interim, someone from our flat had called the police.

Surajit and his boys got to know about it, and they fled. The guard lay bleeding in the ground. It was chaotic, and now, the matter was serious. Both Sejda and Mejda fled from the house and put up in relative's place. The Police knocked in our house, and when they did not find them, they asked them to report at the police station the next day.

Our neighbours were very critical of us. They were calling us "Gundas." However, they were looking at one side of the story. Father was tensed. Abhijit da stood beside us, and Jamai Babu (brother in law) also was there. It was decided that the next day, we would go to the Police Station (PS), and explain the situation.

Next day, they went to the PS along with the Nepali guard. The Inspector was a nice person, and he understood the situation. He asked everyone to sort out the matter amongst us. He also told Mejda and Sejda not to indulge in these things, and they were let off with a warning. Nobody pressed any charges, and the matter was over.

However, it left a bad taste with us. Our neighbours were extremely vocal and were very critical of us. They blamed us for the entire incident. Even after months, when we used to visit Abhijitda's flat, neighbours would talk in hushed voices and point at us and say that these are those guys! It made us feel as if we were some sort of Don or a Gunda.

The second incident was a more serious one which left my father in shock and grief.

One day, we were watching the Benson and Hedges one day match between Australia and India early in the morning. Those days, we were exposed to Channel 9 TV coverage which was out of the world with great commentators like Richie Benaud, Tony Greig and others who made watching cricket worthwhile.

All three brothers were at home. Only Dada had left for his office since his office started early. Father was preparing to go to his office when it all happened.

We saw a series of white Ambassador cars screeching to a halt near our flat and about 4 to 5 people dressed in plain clothes knocked at our flat.

They introduced themselves as CBI, and they had a search warrant for our house and lockers. This was based on a complaint by someone in the bank that father had taken a bribe from some clients. This was unthinkable. A man of such high integrity and honesty was faced with bribery charges. We were stunned. However, we took this in our stride.

The CBI people started searching everything in the flat, every room, and they overturned the mattresses in each bed. They opened all *almirahs* and looked through all books, papers and tables.

It was an exhaustive search. We kept a very nonchalant attitude and continued watching the match!

The CBI people began to realize that the search was futile slowly, and they could not get anything. That was expected. We also did not have much money in the house. We had, maybe, a few thousands!

The CBI people then proceeded along with father to the bank where our locker was. Apart from a few pieces of jewellery, there was again nothing.

After the entire day's proceedings, there was nothing that CBI could find. Later on, I believe that the court quashed the case against my father on the basis of not finding any evidence at all for the allegations made against him.

However, the incident took a toll on my father. That night, we saw him cry for the second time in his life, and he completely broke down.

This was understandable. If my father had wanted to be dishonest, he could have made a lot of money. But, all his life, he was on the path of honesty and integrity. This is something which got engrained with us as well in our future lives. He could not bear the fact that someone would make such a charge. He knew that it was one of his colleagues in his office who would have complained to CBI to take out a personal vendetta against him.

The entire neighbourhood had come to know about the CBI arrest. People talk. I am sure that they would have been thinking and discussing that Mr. Roy must have done something or else why would CBI come and raid their house? However, the good thing was that we never cared to explain the situation to anyone. We comforted father by saying that we knew he was honest. One CBI raid did not change anything, and he must keep his head high in future as well.

Meanwhile, I had passed my higher secondary exam with only 56% marks. I was again in for a shock since I got 36% in English which was one of my strong subjects. It was a two-paper exam out of 200 marks. I was a hundred per cent sure that they had given me marks for only one paper and had not added the marks for the second paper. There was a system of review, but I did not go for it since I was afraid that if the marks got reduced, I would fail. This was unlikely, but I did not want to take the risk since I had lost 2 years already.

Hence, I was left with very poor marks in English and only a second class overall, whereas, I was expecting a first class.

Anyway, I applied for graduation in Political Science in most of the colleges and got through in all of them. However, I chose to stay back in my own St Xavier's College.

Unfortunately, Sejda failed in one of the honours papers in Part II in graduation, and he lost one year. He had to retake that one paper again.

Meanwhile, Mejda had completed his article for his CA and had passed Part 1 of the CA exam. He was now getting ready to complete his Part 2 which was the tougher one.

Father had only 6 months left for his retirement, and only Dada was working. Very soon, the onus would fall on Dada for running the family, though father would get some pension.

Let me now come to music at this stage. I slowly started getting exposed to western music and was soon listening to various western singers. Those days Michael Jackson was becoming the new raging sensation with his video "Thriller" and "Billie Jean" amongst many other chartbusters. He was one of the greatest entertainers who not only sang well but also was a great dancer as well as a composer. Very soon, I was listening to Paul McCartney,

Lionel Ritchie, George Michael, Stevie Wonder, Kenny Rogers, Boney M, Madonna, Bruce Springsteen, Diana Ross and many others.

By this time, we had a 2 - in one cassette player and recorder. I used to listen to these songs on this. My brothers used to jokingly refer to me as "Saheb" because of my interest in western music. Maybe, this was also due to the western influence in our college. However, this did not mean that I did not like Hindi and Bengali music which I used to listen to; as was the case with Hollywood movies.

I started to watch a lot of Hollywood movies in this period and saw many of the best Hollywood movies of the time. I had a very stupid notion earlier that Hollywood movies did not portray the emotions which one could see in the Hindi and Bengali movies. How wrong I was! I was naïve, and it was only when I started watching Hollywood movies did I realise that they were far superior in both content and technology compared to Bollywood and Tollywood. In my view, the content of Hollywood movies is not so great though you get to see some classic movies. But they are far and few in-between.

Father retired from his job finally after a long stint in the bank. Those days, people used to retire from the organisation they joined and did not look at any other opportunities outside. Father had got a few options as well in UAE, but he refused. Maybe, if he had joined there, life would have been different. Even in our times, skipping from one job to another was few and far in between. My eldest brother, after a few initial changes, stuck to Maruti

Udyog Ltd for more than 34 years. I also changed job once after completing 10 years, and my subsequent changes were due to reasons not in my control.

The construction of the new house started. I believe from what I remember that it took almost a year and about 3 lacs to complete a single-storeyed house. I did go through one of the diaries and could make out the immense struggle that father had to undergo to complete this house. He used his entire PF proceeds to build the house, and it was not enough. He had to borrow money from Abhijit da and Jamai Babu again to complete the house. Even then, it was not complete, and there was still work to be done.

Mejda played a major role in supervising the construction of the house. We had not given it to any builder. All the materials like cement, bricks and iron rods were bought by us, and one had to supervise everything. It was a very tough job, and Mejda used to do that. He would cycle every day from out flat in BB Block and go to FE Block where our house was being built. It was far and, it used to take about half an hour in the cycle to reach there. There were only a few buses which used to ply, and they were not very frequent. He used to lose his temper, but we used to take it in our stride knowing that he was putting in a lot of effort.

Finally, we were ready to move to the new house. It had 2 bedrooms. Dada, Boudi and my niece shared one room. The other bedroom was shared by the three of us brothers. Father and Mother used to sleep in the sitting room which had one bed. There was a dining room as well, and a big veranda in the front. A lot of time used to be spent in the veranda, especially, when there were long power cuts, and we had nothing else to do. We would just sit in the dark and have *Adda* (talk sessions).

It was quite a desolate place. I remember that in our lane, there was only one house at one end (our house) and there was another one at the far end. In the entire block, there were very few houses and, in the evening, it used to become completely desolate. One could hear the sound of the jackals as well. Inside the house, we did not have doors in the bedrooms. People used to talk about it, especially, since Dada and Boudi did not have the privacy. I sometimes wonder if our financial position was so precarious that we could not afford to make one door at Dada's bedroom. Maybe not. Finally, the door was made. Even now, the neighbours in Salt Lake talk about it.

Slowly and steadily, there were houses being built, and people started coming into the block. Today, the block is completely filled up and congested. The lanes are filled with parked cars all around.

I started going to college as well. However, the transport was not good with only a few buses plying.

Our block was confusing as was the case with other blocks in Salt Lake and it was difficult to locate houses. I used to find it very difficult to locate our new house once I got down in the bus stand in Karunamoyee Bus Stand which was a couple of kilometres away from our house. In fact, after entering our block, I would inquire with passer-by about our house, and finally, locate it!

The first Durga Puja was being celebrated in our new Para or block. Those days, we used to get our clothes stitched. We would get a couple of shirts and trousers stitched for each of us. We would buy the material from the local shops, and the local tailor would then stitch the same. It was simple, and maybe, not enough. But, we were always content.

Associated with Durga puja closely is the *Mahalaya* which is the start of *Pitri Paksha* when Hindus pay homage to their ancestors, especially, though food offerings. This day has also been made memorable in the lives of Bengalis by one gentleman Birendra Krishna Bhadra for his soaring Sanskrit recitation through a two-hour radio program, *Mahishashur Mardini* (Destroyer of Mahishashur). This was a collection of songs and *shlokas* which used to be broadcasted by All India radio at 4 am. This was started in 1951. It is said that when Birendra Krishna Bhadra first made the recording, he took a bath early in the morning, and then sat for the recording. His voice had so much of passion, love and devotion that it is said that he even cried at the end. When we used to hear it, we all used to get goosebumps. This was not different from anybody else. This became a ritual in the lives of the Bengalis to hear this as part of Durga Puja every year. Though Biren Krishna Bhadra is no more, the recording is played every year on the *Mahalaya* day. Even now, the feeling is no different. Later, in the late 70's, the legendary actor Uttam Kumar would try his hand in this recitation, but he would fail miserably. He could not come anywhere near to what Birendra Krishna Bhadra had delivered.

During the Puja, it was decided that there would be a cultural function, and we would have a "Play." Boudi, as usual, had become very popular in the block, not only with youngsters who used to be very fond of her but also the elderly people who used to like her. She was asked to play a major role in the play. They also decided to cast Dada and me as well. However, the roles were insignificant, and we were both given the roles of servants!

It was great fun during the practice session of the play, and many humorous incidents happened. We used to regale ourselves for a long time after the play was staged. It was a great opportunity to make new friends. Funnily, all people in the play came to be known later by their characters!

Finally, the D - day came. However, that was also fraught with incidents. The first day the play could not be staged since there was a power cut and there was no provision for a generator. Finally, the next day the play was staged, and it was a huge success.

In the years to come, the Puja would happen on a very large scale with a large budget, and the cultural function would be a big affair with the involvement of many people. But, I guess, it has never been the same.

During this time, we got opportunities to make friends with a lot of people. Arun da who was cast as the hero opposite my Boudi became a family friend and continues to be a friend even now. He was a budding artiste. His mother was a famous artiste who used to create magic with needle and thread. She used to make portraits which were lively. She was the recipient of many national and international awards. She started with a small room in a local marketplace, and over a period of time, a double-storeyed art school was inaugurated. It was named as "Rekha Chitram" named after the lady. Arun da has carried the legacy forward and continues to build on that.

Another family who became very close to us after the play was the Sensharma family, and we used to call Sensharma uncle as "Jethu" after the character in the play. He had two daughters who became very good friends not only to Boudi and me but to the entire family.

Very soon, the Khan family came to stay just opposite our house. Khan Uncle was a retired Air Force officer who was suffering from cancer. Their family had one son who was in the Indian army, and he was a Captain. Captain Debasish Khan was a young man who had been part of the Indian Peace Keeping force in Sri Lanka. He used to tell us about his experience in Jaffna island and how difficult was it for them to survive in the island country.

I always had great respect for the armed forces, and especially, for someone so young. He was promoted to the rank of Major very soon. He was very humble and down to earth. He was very pally with me as well. Once, he took me to the army unit in Salt Lake and invited me to the officer's mess where I was introduced to other army officers. I shared a drink with them as well. However, I have now lost touch with him. I am not sure whether he is still part of the Indian army or he has retired. In case he is still part of the Indian army, he would be in a very senior position.

One of my school friends, Abir Ghosh, also went to the Indian Army and was part of Kargil operations. He was posted in Siachen for a couple of years. He also used to tell us about the hardships which they endured in sub-freezing conditions day after day protecting our borders while we could sleep peacefully. He is now a Colonel in the Indian army, and we sometimes meet in our school get-togethers. There were there 3 sisters as well. They also became very good friends. So, I not only had very good friends at our Block but made many good friends at college who continue to be very good friends.

I was very close to Amartya, Basab and David who were my bosom friends, and we used to stay together most of the times. Amartya was a frequent visitor to our house. I always liked the company of female friends and had many of them. They were very good friends - like Rina, Joyeeta, Deboli and Munmun. All these friends would regularly come to our house, and they became very close to my Boudi as well. Our house was always vibrant with people coming whether it was my friends, or my brothers' friends or people from the block. There was never a dull moment.

I was an eternal romantic and liked many girls in college. However, unfortunately, whoever I liked in college used to get married! I am not taking anyone's name here to protect their privacy.

Add to that was my niece who was very naughty and a lively child. I was very fond of her, and so was she. Everyone used to like her. She would play with the children of the maids. Once, she went to their house and had lunch with them at their house. She went missing. Another instance when she went missing, and we could not find her, we started getting panicky. She had run off to the park where the structure was being made for the *pandal,* and she had somehow reached the top of the structure, and she was not able to come down. Finally, we located her, and somehow, managed to get her down.

She started going to a kindergarten school by the name of Little Angels. My father used to take her and bring her back every day from school. Once, on a certain day, when he was unwell, my mother went. My niece (Sumi) was disappointed in not seeing her grandfather, and refused to recognise her grandmother and come with her! It was with great difficulty that the school authorities were convinced that my mother was indeed her grandmother.

Amartya would also come to my house during exams. He was always petrified of exams and would come to our house since he would state that he as not being able to concentrate alone. Once, I remember during one of the exams, he came to my house and was in a great panic since his preparation was not perfect. He asked me to accompany him to his house in Bhadreshwar which is about 35 to 40 Kms from our house. One had to travel on a train from Howrah station, and it used to take about 2 hours to reach his house!

We finally reached his house, studied together and went to college from his house. His house was a beautiful old-fashioned double-storeyed house, and his family was great. His father was in the excise department and had just retired. His mother was very nice, and so were his two elder sisters. They used to love me a lot.

However, there is not too much of a bond between us now. While we are part of a College group which I had created, the magic of the old relationship is no more there.

Sejda had graduated and was doing his one-year stint in hotel management. Mejda was still grappling with his Part 2 in his CA exam. Dada had joined Maruti Udyog and was posted in Kolkata. He was doing well.

I recollect a funny incident which happened while we were all staying together. We had a gentleman by the title of "Bhaduri" who used to stay in our block. He, along with a few people, had come to our house before the pujas to discuss the amount of subscription that was to be fixed for that year. I went over to my Boudi (sister in law) and told her that Jaya Bhaduri's (film actress) father had come to our house, and it was a great chance for her to meet him. My Boudi was so innocent and naïve that with such a straight face she said that she believed me and rushed to the sitting room to meet him. Better sense prevailed, and she probably realised at the last moment of her folly!

No matter what our financial condition was, we would love to eat out once in a while. The only 2 restaurants which we had in Salt Lake was Dandin - a Chinese restaurant and Mishra's which was an Indian restaurant. It was dada who used to treat us.

Coming to food, Kolkata is the food lover's paradise. It is unique in the sense that it caters to all. You can get all kinds of food including Chinese, Indian, tandoori, Bengali, Gujarati and Continental.

Tangra, or the Chinese town, is famous for its Chinese food. We started going there about 25 to 30 years ago. There were only a few. We normally used to go to Kafulok. The food was amazing, and so was the quantity. There were a few others like Kim Ling and Big Boss. Now, there are many more.

The rolls - chicken and egg were our favourites, and I guess, we would get an egg roll at Rs. 2!

Now, Kolkata is spoilt for choices so far as restaurants are concerned, and the variety it has in offer.

During my college days, since I was always short on money, I would have rotis/parathas with buffalo meat which came at Rs. 2 per plate, and it was yum. However, since I had it on a very regular basis, very soon, I was having stomach issues and stomach ache. Since these were small roadside rickety shops, one was never sure about the quality of the meat. Hence, the issue. Post that, I realised that I could not continue with this, and came out of that. I was under medication for a long time.

Sejda cleared his Hotel Management and finally got a job in a Hotel in Rourkela.

Mejda was still struggling and had only a couple of papers to clear his CA exam. But, it was taking a lot of time. Meanwhile, he had joined a Grameen Cooperative Bank and was working there.

I passed my Part 1 Exam securing the 1st Division overall, but I managed to get only 54% in honours subject. Again, I was disappointed in not being able to do better. However, none from my batch secured the 1st class in honours though. Those days securing the 1st class, even in science graduation, was extremely difficult; let alone getting a 1st class in an arts subject.

There was again a debate on whether I should pursue Part 2 or quit. Those days, you were a graduate if you had done your Part 1; though you were only a pass graduate. After much debate and my Dada's insistence, I continued with Part 2. Things were getting a little sticky as father had retired. No one else, apart from Dada, had settled down properly. Hence, the pressure was there.

I continued with my Part 2 in the college. Now, I had only major papers in Political science.

Those days, I used to get Rs 4 on a daily basis. From that, I used to manage my transport, my lunch and save from that money for other activities like watching movies, etc. However, by this time, I had started giving tuitions and was earning Rs. 250 to Rs. 300 per month. It was enough to sustain me. This was required since there were events like birthdays of friends or outings. It was necessary that I could manage them by myself without putting a burden on my brother.

Finally, I became a graduate. However, I could not score a first class and managed to get a decent second class. I had decided that I would not pursue Post graduation and would either go for civil services or get into a job. Many of my friends joined post-graduation course in Calcutta University.

I joined HCL as a trainee salesman to sell computers. We had a full day training on how to sell. In between, they gave us a roll. It had no fixed salary, and there were only incentives. We were introduced to Joy Deep, who was a smart Bengali guy. He was doing brilliantly well in selling computers. Later on, he joined ICICI Bank, and he is in a very senior management position. He gave us tips to sell computers, and what the techniques were, etc. That was my first exposure in sales.

One of the tips was on being compared with competition like Wipro. We were supposed to say "Wipro is a company which makes matchsticks and matchboxes. What would they know about computers?"

My first sales call was to my brothers' friend who needed a computer and wanted to compare it with Wipro. As a cliché, I used the same tip in a very routine manner, and my brother's friend was amused.

When I look back to that incident, I feel very stupid.

Anyway, I started my journey in HCL. I used to travel very far and started making calls in medicine shops, hardware shops and government companies.

However, very soon, I realised that it was not my cup of tea, and I quit the job after a week.

Then I sat for many interviews and exams in many companies, but I could not crack any. However, I was determined to make it. I also started preparing for WBCS and started attending classes for the same.

While I was preparing for WBCS, I sat for an exam for the post of clerk cum typist in Hong Kong Bank. I passed the exam and was called for a group discussion. There were about 40 to 50 people who had been called for the same. I went to the Dalhousie Office of the bank - The Hong Kong Building. I had never seen such a large and beautiful office and a bank. I was totally mesmerised by the glamour of the office.

There was a group discussion which was held. I managed it well, and it was followed by a round of personal interview. Finally, it was over, and we were told that we would be communicated on a later date.

It was getting necessary for me to work now since Dada was now supposed to get transferred to Chandigarh. He would not be in a position to support as he had done earlier.

My niece's birthday was coming on 23rd December. A lot of people had been invited for the same including a lot of my friends.

I sat in the veranda on the 22nd Dec contemplating as to how nice it would be to get the appointment letter before the birthday, and the same would become special.

Can you believe it? There was the courier who rang the bell and handed over an envelope from HSBC. Behold, it was the appointment letter from HSBC with joining date from 1st January 1990 with a salary of Rs. 2000!

This marked the end of one journey and the start of another one. It marked the end of childhood and the beginning of a journey with responsibility. It marked the end of a carefree life with no worries, an uncomplicated life, and heralded the beginning of a life with worries, responsibilities and complexities. The childhood which we traversed in our lifetime would never come back.

When I look back on this journey of our childhood, it was one hell of a journey. I am sure that very few would have been to as many cities, as many schools and as many houses. My childhood journey included travelling to 9 cities, 8 schools, 10 houses, innumerable friends, fantastic memories and a whirlwind journey.

I can bet that very few would have had this varied and interesting a childhood that we had. We did not have the money or the luxuries. What we had was contentment, happiness with small things in life and a great experience.

I also do not know as to how many of you will read this or will find this interesting. I am sure that people in our age group from 40's to 60's would be able to relate it to their childhood. People in the age group in their teens, and from 20's to 40's, would know that life is not about smartphones, I phone and the internet. It is more about being happy with small things and being contended. It is not just connected, it is about friendship and bonding with parents and siblings.

We all are in a hurry to grow up, become an adult, start working and earn. In the process, we ignore our childhood. Before long, we realise that it is gone, and it would never to come back again. Life would not give you another chance to go back to your childhood. Even today, we relive our childhood, and we always feel happy remembering those days. As I said, people in the age group of 40 till 60 had a similar kind of childhood. It is evident when we talk to each other.

So, enjoy it while it lasts, savour it and do not hurry. You will have enough time to earn, to work and to do all the things that you want to do in your adult life. Even when you reach adulthood, do not lose the child inside you.

CPSIA information can be obtained
at www.ICGtesting.com
Printed in the USA
BVHW031435160119
537984BV00001B/19/P

9 781644 299340